A SAMPLE ANTHOLOGY

Edited by:
Charles Kelley

Circle City Publishing presents:

FUN SIZE
A Sample Anthology

Edited by:
Charles Kelley

© 2020

Circle City Publishing

ALL RIGHTS RESERVED. This book contains material protected under International and Federal Copyright Laws and Treaties. Any unauthorized reprint or use of this material is prohibited. No part of this book may be reproduced or transmitted in any form or by any means, electronic or mechanical, including photocopying, recording, or by any information storage and retrieval system without express written permission from the author / publisher.

This is a work of fiction. Names, characters, businesses, organizations, places, events and incidents either are the product of the author's imagination or are used fictitiously. Any resemblance to actual persons, living or dead, events, or locales is entirely coincidental.

Cover design by Steven Hayslett

ACKNOWLEDGMENTS

Special thanks to all of the authors who took the time and effort to contribute to this anthology. Without their imaginations, this project wouldn't be possible. Literally.

Also, thank you to all of the readers. Your support is what keeps us going. Our hope is that you will enjoy all of the following stories, and have nine new authors to be a fan of.

CONTENTS

October in Red – Patrick J. O'Brian..................1

The Lost Warriors – Cait Marie....................40

Horsepower – Charles Kelley.......................66

A Beast Forged – Christian Scully..................86

Arcadis Meets Nokon – George Kramer........123

Tea Party – Adam K. Moore.......................151

Pygmalion – Jason Cobalt..........................179

Blood Dragon: The Search Begins

– Katheryn Schwarz.................................205

You Win, You Lose – Ben Oneal..................249

About the Authors.....................................303

About Circle City Publishing........................315

October in Red
Written by: Patrick J. O'Brian

Steve Deidrick harbored thoughts of killing his sister on her wedding day.

Figuratively, of course, because he couldn't believe she decided to hold her wedding the weekend before Halloween, in such a dangerous place.

Looking at Indiana's West Baden Springs Hotel wouldn't evoke images of blood flowing down the lobby stairs, but locals weren't the only people who knew about its recent indiscretions. Completed in 1902, and renovated in recent decades, the hotel was centered in a few battles of both the legal and bloody persuasions.

Unable to unwind, despite the luxurious settings and most of his family staying on the grounds, Deidrick drank a Bud Light before everyone lined up for the ceremony. He slid the empty bottle into a trash receptacle before meeting his wife of twelve years across the brick driveway near the hotel's grand lobby.

"You okay?" Tera asked as they strolled in the garden toward the white seats set up for the wedding.

Nearly five o'clock now, the sun remained in the sky, and Deidrick heard his stomach growl because they hadn't eaten since breakfast.

"Fine," he answered, wishing Melanie hadn't scheduled her wedding on the same weekend as his birthday.

September proved impossible, she'd said, because the resort held a vintage-themed weekend that brought in tourism, booking too many rooms for the wedding party to stay on the grounds. Deidrick didn't care that baseball players dressed in vintage wool uniforms and men carving art out of tree trunks with chainsaws created such a draw. He wanted a September wedding so he could have his birthday weekend to finally do something enjoyable in October.

About to turn forty, Deidrick didn't typically celebrate birthdays, particularly after his stint in the Army, but the military taught him life couldn't be taken for granted. After several discussions with his sister about his feelings on the subject, she promised him an unforgettable birthday, but after the wedding date changed, she vowed to make it up to him.

Living in Noblesville, a suburb of Indianapolis, Deidrick worked in security for a tech company. Not savvy with technology by his own admission, he supervised a group of men and women who guarded the building and its contents. Now the second-in-command of the security department, Deidrick remained proficient in firearms and hand-to-hand combat. While his job sounded fulfilling to most, it wasn't what they envisioned. Deidrick didn't prevent terrorists from storming the grounds and forcing their way into some computer saferoom. No, he monitored employees through monitors, and on their computers, to ensure they didn't leave with trade secrets at the end of each workday. He longed for something a bit more exciting and exotic, which he certainly wouldn't experience this particular weekend.

"You seem a little tense," Tera prodded.

He hadn't spoken to her much about his disappointment regarding the wedding date, but he'd given his sister an earful a few times.

"I'm good," he said. "This place is incredible."

Both took their seats in the second row. For the money his sister's new family paid to rent the garden area and book numerous rooms in the hotel, Deidrick expected more than white plastic folding chairs and a flower-covered arch. Because the hotel also hosted the reception, they took care of the décor and food as well. He hoped his son and daughter chose to elope when thoughts of marriage entered their minds.

"Do you believe everything Tommy said

about this place?" Tera asked as the ceremony's start drew near.

"About the murders? Well, he would know, wouldn't he?"

Tera spoke of her brother, a detective with the state police, who had access to a variety of case files from when numerous murders took place on the hotel grounds. During a few family gatherings he'd provided descriptions of the murder victims after the fact. Although a few people allegedly posed as the killer back in the day, the people always wore a cloak and a dark mask to give the illusion of the grim reaper committing murder. His weapon of choice, at least part of the time, was a scythe.

Thankfully, the ceremony lasted less than half an hour. Between the sunny day and warm fall temperatures, Deidrick felt beads of sweat run down his face and neck. They eventually slid beneath his dress shirt, feeling like miniature icicles beneath the gray suit he wore that might as well have been a winter coat. Wearing a white shirt with a striped tie containing blue, black, and charcoal coloration, he hadn't strayed too far from conservative attire.

Given the choice between a 1921 Ford Model T and a horse and carriage ride, his sister opted to travel around the hotel grounds in the carriage with her husband. Deidrick felt reasonably certain the first option wasn't provided directly by the hotel, but rather a local owner of vintage cars who charged a fee for couples who wanted the full vintage experience. People who weren't even affiliated with the wedding stopped to snap pictures or create a video of the wedding with their phones. Deidrick stepped aside several times to avoid being part of someone's digital catalog.

Following the ride, everyone gathered inside the lobby area for the reception, which appeared closed off to the general public. Normally, guests checked in at the large front desk, but a single booth remained open facing the atrium along the opposite wall to assist regular guests. Deidrick might have felt a bit special, except that people kept peeking around the black cloth barriers put up between the lobby and the doorways. Deidrick supposed after the wedding date was moved, renting out the entire hotel was no longer an option.

He couldn't argue that the hotel proved as beautiful as writers declared in articles and blogs, but something about the checkered history nagged at him. If a dozen or so murders occurred on the grounds, or nearby, how could such a place stay in business? Many of the stories his brother-in-law told him weren't revealed to the public, at least not in detail, which might explain part of the success. He supposed riches went a long way towards keeping certain facts from reaching the newspapers, and perhaps the local police didn't want to discourage tourism. Money raked in by the resort's casino certainly benefited the county, including all facets of its government.

Deidrick stayed through the first dance

and the best man's toast before he needed to use the restroom down the hall. Having downed two beers since the reception started, he felt the call of nature during the toast. He managed to dance with his wife, though he felt uncomfortable in his nether regions the entire time.

"I'm about to explode," he commented to her at the end of the dance. "I'll be back in a few."

She responded with a grin, knowing him all too well after a dozen years of marriage.

Walking down the hall, Deidrick discovered the corridors mirrored the hotel's round shape, constantly curving. He'd barely laid eyes on his room, because he and Tera ran behind, arriving just before the ceremony began. Deidrick barely found time to check in, running his bags up to the room before grabbing his sport coat and heading downstairs.

Stepping into the restroom, he discovered even it appeared lavish with tile, fresh paint, and amenities near the sinks. At least eight urinals lined the wall with an equal number of stalls across from them. Deidrick chose one in the middle, unzipped his pants, and relieved himself with a throaty sigh as he looked to the ceiling. When the restroom door opened, he didn't look over until a man in a charcoal-colored suit chose a urinal only two down from his own. A cursory glance indicated a man in his early fifties with a fringe of gray hair and a full goatee obviously needed a bathroom break just as badly.

Deidrick didn't recognize him from the wedding party.

"Part of the wedding?" the man asked as Deidrick zipped his pants.

"Yeah. My sister got married."

"Ah," the man said with a nod. "Congratulations."

"Thanks," Deidrick answered, though he dwelled on his birthday taking place the next day with nothing exciting in the works.

"That didn't sound enthusiastic," the stranger noted as he pulled up his zipper.

Before he could think of an answer that didn't sound selfish, Deidrick noticed an employee badge clipped to the front pocket of the man's suit when they turned to face one another.

"You work here?" he asked instead.

"Security," the man answered.

Deidrick read the man's name badge quickly before making eye contact.

Craig Jennings.

"Me, too," Deidrick revealed. "I've heard rumors about this place over the years. Even read a few police reports. How much of it is true?"

Jennings walked over to one of the five sinks, pumping liquid soap into his hands before giving them a warm water rinse. Once he swiped a fancy paper towel from the perfectly aligned stack beside the sinks, Jennings provided a cagy grin.

"I'm afraid the rumors are greatly exaggerated," he said, drying his hands and discarding the paper towel in the nearby receptacle.

"But you were here during some of the events," Deidrick pushed. "I recognize your name from some of the files."

Jennings eyed him suspiciously.

"How did you get your hands on case files?"

"I know some people in law enforcement," Deidrick answered vaguely.

Jennings didn't say anything, as though he thought perhaps Deidrick was fishing for information.

"What did the files say?" he asked after a moment, opening the door for Deidrick as the sounds of music and laughter echoed throughout the atrium, reaching them.

"Well, they didn't cover everything that happened here, but some of the stuff that happened in Bloomington."

"Ah," Jennings said with a knowing smile. "Some investigators came down here back in the day, and ever since the rumors have spread."

"Your boss's wife was murdered," Deidrick said from recollection. "He was their prime suspect for a while."

"My boss is a good man," Jennings said firmly. "He's dealt with some disillusioned people over the years who wanted his money, or this property. Enjoy your reception."

Jennings walked away before Deidrick could follow up with additional questions, or apologize. He didn't want to pester the man, but curiosity ate away at his brain. Though he never sought to join a police department, Deidrick's mind tracked in a similar way to police officers and detectives. Perhaps exploring the hotel's sordid past felt more interesting than the reception, but he couldn't explain why he wanted to know more.

He returned to the reception, staying another two hours as darkness overtook the nearby sunken garden where the columns, chairs, and flower arrangements faded from sight. Inside, the celebration continued with the usual cheesy dances, a few intoxicated comments that couldn't be taken back, and people changing to less formal attire over time. Deidrick bore witness to the events around him, drinking a few more beers and slow dancing with his wife twice before she told him she wanted to go use the hot tub and relax.

"I'll be upstairs in a bit," he commented before she bent over to kiss him.

"Take your time. Your sister only gets married once."

"Maybe," he commented under his breath.

He withstood only another fifteen minutes or so before he spoke with Melanie and her groom, congratulating them and saying he'd see them later, or in the morning. He also spoke with his mother and father, who attended with their spouses. They divorced when Deidrick was still in high school, each of them eventually remarrying during his time in the military. He tried to avoid showing public favoritism to either pair, so he spoke only briefly to each couple before exiting the lobby.

Instead of heading directly upstairs, however, Deidrick made a lap around the first floor, finding only one store open, and a bar that served food a few doors down. He saw a few offices around the bend, wondering if Craig Jennings continued to work late. Feeling reasonably certain the man was actually the head of security at the hotel, Deidrick questioned why anyone with clout would work hotel security during the weekend. Such hours were typically assigned to pimple-faced teenagers or interns because the hotel wasn't at risk. The casino down the road, on the other hand, maintained a full roster of adult security members who wore uniforms mirroring those of police officers.

Pressing the up button for the elevator when he reached it, Deidrick inserted his room keycard once he stepped inside, choosing the fifth floor button. His journey upward proved rather short, and as he exited the elevator, the sounds of music and laughter along the first floor were replaced with eerie silence. Not a soul passed him along the curved hallway as he gazed at each door, looking for room 524, which ended up being halfway around the curved hallway from the elevator.

Sighing aloud, he pulled the keycard from the right front pocket of his dress pants, prepared to insert it into the door when he stopped short, noticing the door was ajar about an inch. Pocketing the card, Deidrick discovered the security bar on the other side of the door kept the door from automatically shutting. He slowly pushed it inward, wondering why Tera would leave the door unsecured as he stepped into a darkened bedroom.

"Tera?" he called softly, unsure if she might be sleeping.

He couldn't imagine she'd used the hot tub on the ground floor and returned so soon, so something felt extremely out of place to him. Flipping on a light switch, he brought the room to life, seeing the bed still made with their luggage on either side. Deciding to check the bathroom to clear the entire room, Deidrick walked over to the nearly closed door, seeing a warm glow from within the room.

Drawing closer, Deidrick pushed the bathroom door the rest of the way open, seeing an orange flicker illuminating the walls and glass shower stall in the otherwise dark room. This time he didn't turn on the lights because his attention was grasped the moment he rounded the corner. Spying a jack-o-lantern on the floor, a candle burning from its gutted interior, the triangles cut to form a face in the vegetable were turned toward a focal point. A dark liquid shimmered atop the tile floor, and as Deidrick slowly drew closer, he saw a human form inside the claw-footed tub with one leg dangling over the edge. Horror gripped him as he remembered the case files describing the murder of a woman where a jack-o-lantern was placed just outside of her bedroom.

He sensed danger as his eyes took in the spectacle of his wife, lying in the bathtub with blood oozing over the tub, onto the floor. Her eyes remained permanently open, focused upward on the ceiling, as her head assumed an unnatural angle. She wore a robe, also covered in blood, as though the killer took her by surprise when she exited the shower, or returned from the pool area downstairs where the hot tub was located.

Feeling numb, Deidrick slowly backed out of the room, knowing not to touch the crime scene, but mentally fumbling to determine his next move. He sucked in some nervous breaths before taking a look around, wondering if the killer dared stay in the area. Once in the main bedroom, finding no danger nearby, Deidrick plucked his cell phone from his back pocket. He tried calling 911, but his phone provided a series of beeps and an artificial voice indicated his call could not be completed. Now he felt more unnerved, and his breathing came in heaves, forcing him to concentrate and make certain he didn't hyperventilate as he reached for the complimentary phone atop a small table.

Dialing the number for the front desk labeled on the receiver, Deidrick listened to two rings before a young lady picked up on the other end.

"This is Laura," she said. "How may I help you?"

"Laura, I need you to call the police," Deidrick answered, fighting to keep his voice calm, hearing his words quiver when he spoke. "There's been a murder."

"Mr. Deidrick? Are you safe?" she questioned, obviously having information about the room's renter in front of her.

"I think so," he answered, looking up from the phone and seeing no immediate danger. "It's my wife. My cell phone couldn't call out."

"I'm calling for police and an ambulance," Laura assured him. "I'm also sending security up to you. Please stay where you are."

"Okay," Deidrick answered, hanging up the phone.

Standing in place momentarily, Deidrick started toward the bathroom, but didn't want to disturb any evidence, or view the horrific sight of his murdered wife a second time. Instead, he paced the main room, wondering in the back of his mind if he should simply wait in the hallway. After all, he'd seen no one else on their floor all day.

Feeling helpless and inadequate, Deidrick waited what felt like an eternity for a call, or someone to arrive. He stuck his head outside the door twice, looking both ways down the hall to find no sign of another human being. When he returned the second time, he saw his suitcase on the other side of the king-size bed. Serving as a reminder that he chose *not* to bring a firearm to the hotel, he regretted the decision because he wanted to hunt down the killer personally.

Weaponless or not, he decided to take action, darting into the hallway as the sound of a gunshot and a man yelping in pain reached his ears.

Too late, he thought, figuring the killer had struck again as he ran along the curved hallway in the direction of the disturbance.

When he rounded the first bend, he spied a man slumped against the outer wall, a bloody spot in his pressed shirt beneath his sport coat. Deidrick quickly ran to his side, looking around for the attacker and finding no one.

"Jennings?" he asked, recognizing the security director who turned to look at him, struggling to breathe due to the wound along the left side of his abdomen.

Deidrick couldn't see much of the wound because of the blood still oozing outward, but he thought he caught a glimpse of reddish innards through the hole in the shirt.

"He got me with some kind of sickle," Jennings said as he grabbed the flaps along the front of Deidrick's suit with his left hand, staining them with blood. "Came out of nowhere."

In his other hand, he held a firearm that he'd obviously discharged during whatever struggle ensued. He looked up to Deidrick, swallowing hard.

"I'm pretty sure I missed," the man confessed, his words growing sluggish and slurred. "Maybe you can do better."

He lifted the sidearm, handing it to a reluctant Deidrick, who couldn't fathom the carnage happening around him. Being a curious observer on the grounds felt harmless, adventurous even, but being thrust in the middle of a life and death struggle didn't feel entirely real.

"Did your people call 911?" he asked the security director.

"Yeah," Jennings answered, clutching his injury with both hands to apply pressure. "He went back the other way, toward the elevator."

"Fuck," Deidrick muttered, standing with the gun firmly grasped in his right hand. "You going to be okay?"

"Not sure," Jennings answered weakly. "Nothing you can do for *me* though. Just watch your back and shoot that fucker."

Deidrick gave a nod and walked down the hall, looking for any activity. He heard and saw nothing as he returned to his room just long enough to grab a towel hanging on a chair outside of the bathroom. Sucking in an apprehensive breath, he looked at the bathroom door, not daring to enter the crime scene again. Turning quickly, he jogged down the hall with the towel, finding the security director in the same position, either unconscious or dead.

"Can you hear me?" he asked as he knelt down.

Deidrick placed the towel at the site of the wound without looking too closely at the blood, putting Jennings' hands atop the cloth. The man groaned lightly, and Deidrick wasn't certain anything could be done to save him if an ambulance didn't arrive soon.

"Hang in there," he said, standing to

pursue the killer, wondering if the person simply returned to the first floor where he might blend in with any number of guests.

He hoped the incoming first responders knew where to go, but Deidrick didn't want them walking into a trap. With no means of communicating to the outside world at his disposal, he started down the hall, taking only a few steps before he found the answer to his most pertinent question.

Standing before him, beside the open stairwell, the killer stared at him, holding a short scythe with a manageable curved blade, partly covered in blood. Questioning the events unfolding around him for the briefest of moments, Deidrick hesitated just long enough for the killer to dart up the stairs as he took aim and fired two shots that sailed into the curved hallway beyond the small parlor, opposite the stairwell.

"Fuck," Deidrick muttered, taking chase in time to hear footsteps ascending the stairwell.

Only one floor remained, and much of the

wedding party had reserved the sixth floor. In the recesses of his mind, Deidrick wondered if the killer targeted him personally, or his family, for some sick, twisted reason.

More furious than concerned for his own safety, Deidrick raced up the stairs, taking just half a second to glance on either side of the doorway before entering the sixth floor hallway. A handful of rooms and the large suite his sister and her husband rented for the evening occupied much of the level, but Deidrick hadn't laid eyes on the area yet.

Holding the gun in a ready position, Deidrick quickly realized he had the floor to himself, with the exception of a man who just took two lives. He stalked the floor in a clockwise direction, vigilantly searching for the killer, passing several closed doors without spying any clues.

He reached the main door to the suite, finding the largest parlor in the hotel just outside, as though one might host a tea party or some function with the multiple seats and tables. Without much thought, he passed the closed door, but a thumping noise inside drew his attention, causing him to pivot towards the main entry. Reaching the door in a few steps, he held the gun firmly as he turned the knob with his left hand, finding the interior enshrouded in darkness.

Not knowing what to expect, Deidrick didn't want to terrify his sister, or another family member, by charging in with a firearm, but he preferred not to be gutted by a scythe, either. Scanning the main room with his eyes, Deidrick saw a living area complete with seating and a large television, a conference table behind that, and a kitchen to the side of the large table. Thanks to the wedding party, the room was filled with balloons and decorations, which only served to distract him from locating the source of the noise.

He carefully navigated around the furniture, seeing light sources from other rooms that barely illuminated the suite. At least two bedrooms completed the vast area that occupied nearly a third of the hotel's top level. Not finding any people or fallen items in the main area, Deidrick stepped into the bedroom to his right, finding a huge bed complete with jacquard coverings. He inspected the bathroom and two closets, finding nothing of interest in either area.

Tempted to skip searching the other bedroom and return to the hallway, Deidrick stepped into the main suite room, finding a cloaked figure standing on the other side of the conference table. Holding the scythe between his two hands, the killer didn't appear fazed by the fact that Deidrick gripped a gun in one hand. Perhaps surviving the encounter with Jennings made him bold, or he possessed some knowledge Deidrick wasn't privy to.

Raising the gun, he prepared to fire, but the masked figure dashed for the door and Deidrick fired twice, failing to lead his target appropriately and missing. He ran out the door, confronted with a scene that made his heart skip a beat as his sister had come to the top floor, likely knowing nothing of the noise from the firearm if she took the elevator. How anyone throughout the hotel couldn't have heard the gunshots puzzled Deidrick, but as the killer grasped his sister in one arm, he held the modified scythe up to her throat with the other.

"Steve, what's going on?" Melanie asked with panic in her eyes.

"Sis, don't make a move. This guy killed Tera and a security guy."

"Oh, my God," she gasped, trying to wriggle free, prompting the killer to clasp her tighter and restrict her movements.

"Easy," Deidrick said, addressing the killer, refusing to lower the firearm. "There's been enough damage done for one day."

In no mood to negotiate after losing his wife, Deidrick felt compelled to take any measures necessary to save his only sibling.

Now the killer began backing away with

his quarry, and Deidrick knew with one simple move of his wrist, the man could run the blade across his sister's throat. Before the cloaked figure could back through the doorway, gaining cover and changing the scenario, Deidrick raised the pistol and aimed at the man's head in one swift motion, pulling the trigger.

His sister moved forward as the man's head snapped back and he dropped to the floor in a heap, obviously dead the moment the trigger was pulled. Pulling her into a hug, Deidrick let the gun drop to the floor.

"You okay?" he asked.

"I am now," she answered as though still in shock.

Both stood awkwardly a moment, and Deidrick wasn't sure what step to take next, since no additional help arrived after Jennings.

"What a terrible day," his sister said, uttering the words before a smile crept across her face. "What a wonderfully terrible day."

Deidrick sensed something amiss when

she spoke the words, and when the cloaked figure on the floor began to stir, he jumped aside a bit and began scrambling for the discarded firearm.

"Whoa!" Melanie said, stopping him from grabbing the gun.

"What's going on?" Deidrick asked as footsteps approached from beyond the threshold and the cloaked figure stood, beginning to remove his mask.

Suddenly everyone from the wedding party showed up, and Tera and Craig Jennings made their way to the front of the pack.

"What the *hell* is going on?" Deidrick asked more emphatically this time. "You're okay?" he asked Tera directly, receiving an affirmative nod.

"Remember a year ago when you said you wanted something special for your big birthday?" his sister asked. "We started planning all of this for you."

"For me?" he asked with a raised

eyebrow. "You scared the shit out of me."

Tera approached him.

"You've always said how boring your job is, so we decided to give you a chance to play hero by incorporating it into the wedding night."

"So no one died, or got hurt or anything like that?" he asked for clarification.

Jennings stepped forward and poked at the innards sticking through his dress shirt.

"All fake," he stated.

"Do you really work here?" Deidrick asked, the initial shock of being pranked beginning to fade.

"I do. Your family rented out the entire place for the wedding and your birthday surprise."

Deidrick bent over to pluck the firearm from the carpeted hallway.

"And this?"

"It shoots blanks," the young man who'd been posing as the killer said.

"Oh, this is Jake," Melanie said. "He's the

stuntman we hired to make this realistic for you."

"*For* me?" he asked incredulously for a second time. "I feel like I've been pranked on some reality show."

His sister walked up and gave him a big hug.

"This was only part of your birthday surprise," she revealed. "We're taking you and Tera to Hawaii with us on the honeymoon."

Deidrick stood in her embrace, stunned momentarily, thinking anything sounded better than staying at the hotel where he'd just been put through hell. When his sister released the hug, he turned to Tera, fighting back a smile.

"You were in on this?"

"The whole time, dear," she said before planting a kiss on his lips. "You always said you wished your job would give you a little more adventure, so we decided to give you a taste."

"A bit excessive," Deidrick argued.

"If your blood wasn't pumping, it wouldn't have been a thrill."

"Someone could've gotten *hurt*."

"That's why we hired Jake," Melanie said.

"I can take a few hits," the stuntman said. "We planned every detail, right down to the blanks, the fake blood, and even jamming your phone so you couldn't call 911."

Deidrick looked out a window to the atrium, seeing guests milling below them.

"The gunshots," he said. "Didn't someone hear them and call the police?"

"Everyone here is in on it," Jennings revealed. "Your sister's groom invited some work friends who posed as guests. The entire hotel is rented out to their party."

"Why did you go along with this?"

Jennings shrugged.

"Mainly to make certain no one got hurt. And because it sounded like the perfect birthday gift for you once they explained it to me."

"I don't know about that," Deidrick said. "It scared the shit out of me."

"But now you've experienced saving the

day," Melanie said, taking his hand. "I shared my special day with you to give you your birthday surprise."

"I guess that does make you an awesome sister," Deidrick concurred.

"We need to get a wedding photo with all of us covered in blood before we get cleaned up!" Melanie said with delight, since everyone wanted a special niche to remember their wedding or reception by.

For his part, Deidrick felt thankful none of the events that just transpired would reach the internet.

Deidrick chuckled, appreciating the effort put forth by his family to provide him with a birthday surprise, beginning to see they wanted to provide him with an experience most people never saw during their lifetimes. Looking down at his shirt, he saw the fake blood staining the garment across his chest. Everyone else in the wedding party began dousing their clothes with fake blood from a few tubes being passed around. Even his parents and their spouses had made their way upstairs to join the festivities. Shaking his head, Deidrick couldn't imagine how he would explain his sister's special day, or their final wedding photo, to friends and family.

***

While the wedding party gathered for their final, bloody photograph, Craig Jennings walked down the hallway, finding a familiar man waiting for him beside the stairwell. Tall and slender, the mustached man wore brown cowboy boots, blue jeans, and a tan button-up shirt, giving the impression he might be heading to a tavern instead of strolling the grounds of a grand resort.

"Mr. Clouse," he said, addressing the hotel owner formally, though his boss never asked him to.

"I'm still not sure why I let you talk me into this," Clouse said, shaking his head.

"For the right reasons," Jennings replied.

"This hotel is never going to lose its stigma unless we play into it. If everyone thinks what really happened here is an exaggeration, or some urban legend, that's all the better for us."

"We've both survived those dark days," Clouse said, the painful memories written on his face.

For his part, Jennings took the life of a murderous person when the grounds were terrorized by several fiends attempting to grasp power and fortune. He remained loyal to Clouse, who provided him guaranteed employment with substantial pay for his service, and his silence on matters in the past.

"You've lost more than anyone," Jennings told his boss.

"While that's true, the past couple years have been a blessing," Clouse said.

Clouse inherited the hotel, along with its cursed history, and after a failed attempt to sell it, decided to keep it as his albatross. For a brief time, he moved his family into the top floor suite, but even a move meant to protect them with hundreds of people in the hotel at any given time backfired. People determined to hurt the hotel owner or his family always seemed to find a way through bodyguards, defenses, and tactics.

In recent years, Clouse kept his family away from the hotel, and trouble seemed to fade, causing the rumors and media frenzy to dwindle.

"The only thing I know is you have one happy wedding party on your hands, boss," Jennings stated. "And we sold out the entire hotel tonight just for them, so business is good."

"If you say so," Clouse responded with a smirk. "Guess I had to see how this scheme of yours unfolded."

"Without a hitch," Jennings said before looking down at his fake injury. "Well, unless you count being gashed with a plastic prop."

Clouse grinned.

"You going to take the rest of the night off?" he asked.

"Thought I might crash here in one of the

extra rooms," Jennings said, speaking of a select few rooms reserved for employees stranded by weather, car troubles, or other issues.

"I'm going home to the family if you've got things under control here."

"I do," Jennings assured him.

"Take care, Craig," Clouse said, turning to leave before swiveling around for one last word. "And if I don't see you before then, Happy Halloween."

Jennings smirked.

"You would have to say that."

Learn more about the series:

What begins as a dream job for Paul Clouse soon turns into a nightmare when his work at the West Baden Springs Hotel is marred by murder and mayhem. He becomes the focus of a murder investigation, and the luxury hotel, being renovated by the company that employs him, is targeted by people who seek to own the grounds at any cost.

Over the years, the motives for the murders become clearer, and those closest to the hotel learn of a dark time in the hotel's history when the rich and powerful set events into motion that benefited only them. Lives are lost in the struggle to keep the hotel from falling into the wrong hands, often at the hands of a person dressed in a dark cloak, assuming the appearance of the grim reaper, using a scythe on innocent victims.

The West Baden Murders Series

chronicles these events, spanning a decade of the weathered hotel being restored and reopened, seemingly never at peace. When the characters think they know the answers, the past rears its ugly head, bringing them additional turmoil and death. Only when they face a threat that endangers the world far beyond their small Indiana town do the survivors begin to understand the danger entrenched beneath them for a century.

The Lost Warriors

Written by: Cait Marie

Chapter 1

His feet slid across the loose gravel as Loxley pulled himself around the corner of a building, nearly dropping the bag hanging from his shoulder. The bay glistened at the bottom of the hill, mere blocks separating him from his escape. Footsteps pounded the cobblestone streets all around. The sound of clanking armor and people rushing to get out of the way echoed off the stone buildings.

Loxley ran down the shadowed, narrow alley, keeping his goal in sight. He glanced over his shoulder to see a dozen of the king's guards trailing behind him. Trying to slow them down, he grabbed onto a stacked tower of crates and shoved it to the ground as he ran by. He was yards from the open docks, where his crew waited for him on the ship.

Or so he thought. As soon as he stepped out of the alley and into the sun, guards came at him from both sides. He turned, looking for a way out, but the men who had been chasing him had also caught up. Guards surrounded him from every direction. With the water ahead as his only option, Loxley took a deep breath and prepared to jump. When he stepped forward, a path cleared among the guards to reveal his crew. Ropes and chains restrained each of them. One guard held a dagger against the throat of his second in command, Briar. Though his crew subtly nodded for him to go, he knew he could never leave them. After all, it was him the guards truly wanted. Slowly, he lowered the bag of stolen goods from his shoulder and raised his hands in surrender.

They grabbed Loxley, bound his hands,

and he and his crew were hauled to the castle dungeons. Loxley was forced into his own cell, separated from the rest by a solid concrete wall and iron bars. The bitter air seeped through his clothes as he sat against the stone wall. With his head in his hands, he ignored questions from the others. They didn't know how they had been caught, but he did. And it broke his heart. The grief was suffocating.

After several hours, guards returned and led Loxley upstairs in chains. He squinted through the brightness as he adjusted to the stark contrast of the dim dungeons below their feet. He expected to be brought to the throne room, where he would inevitably be given a death sentence. Instead, he was shoved to his knees in a small council room. The king sat before him, surrounded by a handful of advisors and his queen beside him.

Loxley stared at the reflective, marble floor until a hand grabbed him by the hair and forced him to meet the eyes of one of his oldest friends. The king stared at him with a hand rubbing his jaw. Afraid of what he would see, Loxley refused to look at the queen.

"Leave us," the king called out to his advisors. One by one they trickled out of the room, and the few remaining guards all stepped back to the nearby wall. When the door shut, the king asked, "Why, Loxley?"

His words sounded sorrowful, but Loxley knew better. From the corner of his eye, he saw the queen fidget in her seat and wring her hands together. He took a deep breath and shook his head at the king. There was no answer he could give that would change the king's mind if it was already made up. He knew that better than anyone.

"Will there at least be a trial for my crew?" Loxley asked.

"No," the king growled.

"Henri." The soft, pleading voice drew Loxley's attention. He finally met her red-rimmed eyes—the gaze of his lifelong best friend. Loxley clenched his jaw and fists.

"I have already decided upon your punishment," King Henri said. Loxley looked to him with a raised brow. "I'm not going to kill you, Loxley. We've been through too much together."

Loxley let out a relieved breath. There was a beat of silence and the king cleared his throat, sitting up taller. "As you know, the fighting across the sea is spreading. Rayerna is gaining too much control. You and your crew will be using your skills in thievery to blend in and gain information. You're a talented swordsman; I can't deny that."

"Well, I was always able to beat you," Loxley mumbled under his breath.

King Henri ignored him and continued, "You are going to serve me for three years, then you will be banished from this kingdom."

Loxley laughed. "How exactly are you going to control two dozen men who want nothing to do with you?"

"Oh, don't you worry about that. All will be

revealed when you set sail tomorrow."

There would be no arguing. Loxley was swiftly dismissed, and a guard stepped forward to force him to his feet. Too soon, he was back in his solitary cell. A silence settled as he conveyed all that the king said to his crew. A few tried to keep the group hopeful, insisting that they'd find a way out of their situation. Reynold, a strong, brooding man, looked to Loxley from across the aisle. He nodded in understanding—there was no escaping this time.

It was late into the night when he heard a soft set of footsteps approaching. Loxley sat against the wall with his knees pulled up and his arms draped over them.

"You shouldn't be here," he whispered, not needing to look up to know who stood there.

"I'm sorry."

He glanced over to find her face lit by the moonlight streaming in from the small window. His chest ached at the sight of the queen's sad eyes. It had been hurting since he entered that church basement—their secret meeting spot—and she wasn't there. When he saw a dozen guards waiting in her place.

For most of their lives, they were inseparable—Loxley, Mariella, and Henri. They met as young children. Mariella was of noble blood, and Loxley's mother worked in her home. Without any other family but his younger sister, the two often went with their mother and played in the gardens while she worked. Mariella befriended them both and introduced Loxley to Henri. They immediately got along, bonding over their love for fencing and history of war.

Henri was still the prince when he discovered Loxley and Mariella's love for one another. His jealousy overshadowed their years of friendship, and he announced his intentions of marrying Mariella and making her the future queen. Loxley had no power over the crown. He came from nothing, barely supporting his mother and sister. As a child, his mother brought them from Rayerna, claiming the need to start her life over. Loxley caught bits and pieces of the story as he grew up. Something about an abusive, wealthy husband. Loxley never pushed for more, and he could not hate her for running.

Mariella married Henri, whose father passed away shortly after. Henri was crowned King of Detmarya and Mariella his queen. She was kept busy, away from Loxley. The kingdom slowly deteriorated under Henri's rule, and Loxley made it his mission to help as many people as he could. That was how he met Briar and Reynold, then the rest of the crew.

After Mariella caught Loxley stealing food from the castle kitchens, she insisted on helping. For months, they had been meeting. She believed in what they were doing—stealing from a selfish king to help those less fortunate. It wasn't until months later that she confessed to still being in love with him.

Agreeing to one last steal, they prepared to leave together and not return. They hired a ship to take them to Rayerna and planned to send for his family once they arrived. He would protect them from whatever monsters haunted his mother there. Except Mariella never showed up. After twenty years of friendship, it was that betrayal that hurt the worst. Worse than the day she told him she would be marrying Henri.

"Why?" He didn't need to clarify.

The queen kneeled as close as she could get. Leaning against the bars, she whispered, "He knew. Henri found out somehow. I think he was having me followed. I thought if I didn't show up, you'd leave, and he wouldn't be able to find you." A tear rolled down her cheek. "I am so sorry, Loxley."

With a sigh, Loxley looked back down at his hands. "I know, Mariella," he told her softly. "I know you are." They sat quietly together, neither speaking. Before she stood to leave, he reached out and gently squeezed her hand. She let out a soft sob, then disappeared into the night as silently as she came.

The next day, they were forced down to

the docks. Heavy clouds filled the sky, reflecting the somber mood of Loxley's men. As they neared the ship that would take them across the sea, they stopped before the king and queen. Beside them, Loxley recognized Henri's mother and younger brother, though it had been years since he last saw either of them.

With a glance to the king, who nodded in approval, his mother stepped forward and pulled out what looked like a deck of large cards. Under her breath, an almost rhythmic chant began as she held the cards up before her. Thunder boomed overhead, and Loxley's eyes snapped up to the queen. She bit her bottom lip with worry. Everyone knew the rumors about the king's mother being a witch—someone who practiced the old ways. Growing up with Henri, Loxley knew how true those rumors actually were. It was why she stayed hidden in the castle away from the public.

"Henri, don't do this," Loxley pleaded. When the king wouldn't say anything, Loxley looked to the queen. "Mariella."

Neither replied. The king's mother continued. As her voice grew louder, her silver hair began to whirl around, and water sprayed up onto the wooden planks. The language was old and unfamiliar. A tugging pressure crushed Loxley's chest. Lightning cracked loudly nearby as she spoke the final words. Loxley fell to his knees, breathing heavily as the weight lifted. He looked to the side to see his crew in similar states.

"Your lives are now tied to these cards," the woman croaked. She walked closer and turned the cards in their direction. A crew member appeared on each one, surrounded by the swirling, gilded letters of the language she used. "So long as your image remains intact, you shall remain whole. Never aging. Never dying."

"You will serve as I said," Henri began. "And no one will be able to defeat you."

To illustrate his point, a guard pulled out a sword. Before anyone could move or say anything, he pierced the blade through Briar's abdomen. Loxley shouted, watching him slump to the ground. He clenched his jaw, then pushed to his feet. Guards grabbed him as he lunged for the king. It took four men to hold him back.

"Patience, Loxley." The king nodded to where Briar lay on the ground.

Loxley watched in wonder as his friend began to rise. Briar pushed himself up and slowly pulled at the hem of his shirt, enough to see his stomach. His skin was smooth beneath the blood. All traces of injury gone.

"What is this?" Loxley asked, looking back to Henri.

"I told you, you are to do my work across seas. We will keep these cards to ensure you fulfill those three years of work. At the end, she will lift the curse. Then you are to leave and never return."

Chapter 2

Dirt sprayed across the sky as a cannonball impacted the hard earth. Briar cursed loudly, and Loxley shook his head with a grin. As his ears rang, he yelled over the commotion, "That one was a little too close for comfort."

Not that it really mattered. Time and time again the curse was put to the test. For three years, they did the king's dirty work. They fought in battles against Rayerna and infiltrated their court, reporting back information to turn the war to their advantage. They even manipulated the kingdom into a treaty with Detmarya. With each victory, the rumors grew of immortal warriors who moved across the land like ghosts. No one knew who they truly were; no one could defeat them. Stories spread, and they became known as the Nihryst.

"The treaty is being signed today," Briar said, ducking beneath a branch. Their small group continued through Shirewood Forest, close enough to the cliffside to see the ships off the coast but far enough into the trees to remain mostly hidden. "Why are Detmaryan ships still firing?"

"Because Henri refuses to back down until that treaty is signed and in his hands," Loxley replied. Louis met his eyes with a sigh. The younger prince had joined them on this final mission days earlier. Behind them, Lord Vonhar huffed and complained as his chains rattled. Unaccustomed to such physical exertion, he struggled through the rough terrain. As one of the lead financers of Rayerna's forces, he was to be traded in return for Detmarya withdrawing. Louis's mouth quirked up on one side, and he shook his head.

With just a few years separating them, Loxley knew the prince well. Despite everything, Loxley still couldn't bring himself to hate him. He was so unlike the king in every way. Where Henri was selfish and cold, Louis was easygoing and caring. He fought in this war against his family's wishes because he truly wanted to help his kingdom.

They reached the edge of the village, where fighting in the streets continued. Shouts filled the air along with the sounds of blades clashing. Loxley turned to Briar to go over the plan once more. They might be immortal, but their prisoner and the prince were not. And both needed to get to the castle in one piece. They needed to make it through the chaos that was unfolding before them. Briar pointed to a clearing that led to an abandoned side road.

The castle could be seen in the distance—a straight shot once they reached the street. Briar had been right in choosing this path. They left the fighting behind and made their way south. Lord Vonhar walked in the middle of the group, both to protect him and to keep him from running. Loxley forced the prince to walk beside him as well.

Yards from the gate, the shouting increased. Loxley held up a hand, signaling the group to stop at the end of the road. They stuck close to the wall, but there was no hiding in the bright midday sun. Loxley peeked around the corner of a brick building to the main road beyond. The street was so congested with fighting, fallen bodies, and debris that he could not tell which side had the advantage.

The tall, gilded gate stood closed, diagonal from where they hid. Loxley took a deep breath, looked from Briar to Louis with a nod, then sprinted toward the gate with them on his heels.

He heard the whirring noise before understanding what was happening. The volume increased as it grew closer, but by the time it registered, it was too late.

"Get down!" Loxley shouted back at his men. He dove for cover against the towering wall that surrounded the palace grounds just as the world went tumbling around him.

The cannon hit the closest building, sending bricks showering to the street. Loxley covered the back of his head as debris fell. When it settled, he choked on the thick, dirt-filled air. He looked through the clouds of dust for his crew.

"Briar," he barely managed to shout.

"Over here," Briar called out. Loxley spotted him crouched over a still figure. His stomach sank, and he ran toward them.

"No!" Loxley fell to his knees beside the prince. Louis lay unmoving, half buried under the rubble. Blood spilled from a deep gash in his head and a brick sat next to him. Loxley felt for a pulse, for a breath, but there was nothing.

After three years, the crew was used to the sight of death. It barely fazed them anymore. But this struck Loxley in the heart. Louis had been like a younger brother to him for the better part of their lives.

Loxley clenched his jaw then stood, looking for the rest of his crew and Lord Vonhar. The prisoner stood a few feet away, fully intact. They needed to keep moving, he knew that. He refused to leave the prince, though. Squatting down, he hauled Louis over a shoulder. The fighting in the street had quieted. A good portion of the soldiers affected by the impact. There was no trouble reaching the gate now. It had even jarred open during the commotion.

Chapter 3

Loxley waited for the explosion—the eruption he knew to expect. But it didn't come. The king stood looking down at his brother. His heavy breathing and clenched fists the only indication of the storm brewing within. Anger radiated off him, but he did not shout. He didn't say a word.

Lord Vonhar had been escorted to a holding cell in the dungeon until he would be moved to the king's ship. The advisors and noblemen had been excused from the meeting chamber, as had the Nihryst. The king and queen of Rayerna followed, mumbling condolences and averting their gaze as they passed Loxley. They closed the door, leaving just him and Henri.

"Henri," Loxley whispered. He took a step forward, and to his surprise, the king did not retreat when Loxley placed a hand on his arm. "I'm sorry. There was nothing I could do. If the cannons hadn't—"

"Don't," Henri hissed, cutting him off. He turned to look at Loxley. "Don't you dare blame me for my brother's death."

"I wasn't."

"He chose to follow your group of criminals." Henri snatched his arm away and took a step back. Looking back down at Louis, he whispered, "I should've just killed you."

"Why didn't you?"

"You know why."

Mariella. Somewhere deep inside the cruel king was the caring friend he grew up with. Despite everything, Henri did truly care for her. They both loved her. That's what caused the rift between them in the first place.

Loxley just nodded then made his way to the door.

"Be ready to leave by sunrise." Henri's tone wasn't unkind, which surprised Loxley more than the words themselves.

He glanced back with one hand on the doorknob. "Where will you send us?"

The crew had talked about their different options—what they'd do once the curse was lifted and they were banished from Detmarya. Most of the crew had only ever lived there until this punishment.

"Tugora."

Loxley knew little of the island famously known for its pirate inhabitants. It was nothing more than a stopping point for most. It might not be home, but it would give him a place to start over.

"What about my mother and Willa?" Images of his younger sister flashed through his mind.

"They will be left alone," Henri said.

"Thank you," Loxley mumbled before turning to leave. He would write to them the first chance he got and have them join him. He believed the king, though; they would be safe. Henri always had a soft spot for them.

*****

The sea lapped at the sides of the ship the next morning. The treaty had been signed, and the king ordered a ceasefire. A handful of ships sailed south, away from the wreckage of war. With the Nihryst sailing to Tugora, their journey was much longer than the navy heading home. After a few days, none of the other ships were visible.

They travelled along the west coast of Detmarya. Loxley often found himself on the deck, watching the mountainous landscape drift past. He prayed to the stars to keep his family safe until they were once again united. Farther south they sailed. Days turned into weeks, and the air slowly warmed around them.

On what was to be the last leg of the trip, they were intercepted by a large ship with blue and green flags flapping in the wind. Briar met Loxley's gaze as they stood at the railing. He shrugged, not understanding either. Soldiers boarded their ship, followed by the king, queen, and the king's mother. Loxley sighed at the sight of her. It would all be over soon. They would be free.

Chapter 4

The silence should have been their first clue.

When the crew was ordered to go up on deck, that they had arrived and needed to get to the rowboats, they should have known something was wrong. Tugora was not a large city, but according to the information Loxley had gathered, he knew it had docks wide enough for dozens of ships. There would be no need to row in.

They reached the deck and looked out to a small landmass in the near distance. An island that most certainly was not the lively Tugora he had heard about. An island that appeared to be uninhabited when they reached the shore.

The two dozen members of the Nihryst were all but tossed onto the warm sand. Dread filled Loxley as he took in their surroundings. There was nothing—no town or people. Just tall palm trees with tropical plants creating a small, dense forest.

When the other boats began heading back to the ship, Loxley turned around. "Henri, why? You promised!"

"This island is called Cyfrin. It isn't marked on any maps. No one will find you here," he explained. "I vowed to set you free. I made no such promise of making it easy for you."

"The curse?"

The king sighed and looked to his mother,

who shook her head. The guards pulled the oars back, starting to row.

"No!" Loxley shouted. He ran forward into the tide. The water crashed against his thighs as he yelled for them to stop, but the remaining soldiers drew their swords. They blocked his way to the king. He did not have his sword. His weapons, as well as his crew's, had all been taken when they boarded the ship weeks earlier. The royal family and its guards rowed out farther.

"For three years, you killed the enemy and protected our people. You saved hundreds, but you did not save one." Loxley closed his eyes with regret as the king's mother spoke. "You failed to save my son."

"We couldn't save him. There was nothing we could do," Loxley said. He looked to Henri, silently apologizing, then to Mariella. She shook and lowered her head.

The witch went on as if he hadn't said anything. "Now you will suffer here, alone for all eternity."

Shouting started around Loxley as her words sank in. She wasn't lifting the curse.

"When the cursed become mere legend," the queen's mother began as she held up the cards for them to see, "and a true believer found, the key to their freedom will be presented by the descendant. Only when forgiveness is fully given and the other half found, will an act of true love set their souls free. The curse shall be paid for and lifted where it all began."

Loxley stopped and stared. Briar and Reynold approached, standing on either side of him. They watched as their salvation rowed away. The Nihryst were being abandoned on an unknown island.

They were to live there as immortals forever.

Learn more about the series:

Find out what happens when Princess Adalina, the descendant of Henri and Mariella, goes in search of Loxley and his crew a century later in Cait's debut novel, *The Lost Legends: The Nihryst Book 1*! Available March 18, 2020. Books two and three of the Nihryst Series are tentatively scheduled for release later in 2020.

Horsepower
Written by: Charles Kelley

Ever hear about how important it is to surround yourself with good people and avoid bad influences? Let me put it this way: growing up around an outlaw motorcycle club comes with a lot of implications. It implies that I probably didn't have quality supervision. Hell, forget *quality* supervision, it implies that I probably didn't even have *adequate* supervision.

My name's Will McGee, and I think you could say I've pretty much beat the odds to get where I am today. Let me share a little about my background, and you can reach your own conclusions.

"Go get me some smokes," Lee, my old man, yells from the living room at the other end of the house.

I ignore him until he yells again.

"Hey! I need some cigarettes. Run down to the Gas N' Go and pick some up for me."

I step out of my room and am instantly assaulted with the distinct smell of weed and booze. "Oh, sorry. I thought you had me confused for a prospect or something there for a minute. I don't have any money. Plus I'm only sixteen," I say, pretending like this isn't a normal scenario.

Dad pulls a ten-dollar bill from a wad of cash in his pocket and flings it on the coffee table that sits in front of the couch he's currently occupying. White powder scatters from being displaced by the currency. I snatch the bill and shake it off in an attempt to hopefully ensure I don't get a contact high from any residual cocaine clinging to the paper.

"I got you a free car. The least you can do is run some errands when I need somethin'," he responds.

I bound out of the house toward the driveway, dodging dad's 1948 Harley-Davidson Panhead sitting right outside the front door, and reach for the door handle of my recently acquired first car. Through dad's connections in the Kings of Chaos Motorcycle Club, he was able to secure this car from one of the other members. Since they rely on their bikes ninety-five percent of the time, they don't have much use for a cage, or car, as it's referred to outside the biker world. All I had to do was be a gopher whenever the club needed something and the car was all mine. I didn't have any other options, so it was a pretty sweet deal for me.

The car, a 1978 Mustang II, could've been cooler looking, but with some notable upgrades it was a beast mechanically, so I couldn't complain too much. Oh yeah, and it was free. I slid into the bucket seat and turned the key in the ignition, bringing the 302-cubic inch, 5.0 liter V-8 to life. While the Mustang II is a black eye for the reputation of the iconic pony-car, I forgot to mention mine was a Cobra II. Now the specs of this car were a joke when it came off the production line, but as already mentioned, thanks to some considerable modifications, the same can't be said of this particular model anymore. With the small frame and light weight of the vehicle, the performance package made this car a rocket in a straight line. Just don't ask me to take any turns at speed.

In no-time-flat I'm parking in one of the few designated parking spots in front of the only convenience store in Rough River Falls. I can't help but notice two Harley-Davidsons sitting at the gas pumps and instantly recognize that they belong to Griz and RJ, a couple of the Kings that are basically extended family. RJ serves as the MC's Vice Prez, while Griz is a long-time full-patch member.

I step up to the counter inside the Gas N' Go and ask for a pack of cigarettes. The clerk casts me an annoyed expression, knowing full-well I'm not old enough to purchase tobacco products. Sure, technically they could get in trouble with the excise police if they ever got caught, but that's the beauty of being in Small-town, USA; everybody knows everybody else and excise has bigger fish to fry than waste their time in Nowhere-ville, Kentucky.

"What's up, Will?" RJ asks, approaching from the rear of the store with Griz, toting a six-pack in each hand.

"Hey guys, just getting some smokes *for dad*," I say, emphasizing the last two words so the clerk hears them loud and clear. "Gonna be able to get those back to the clubhouse?" I glance at the beer in their hands. "I hope you're not expecting me to mule them around for you."

"Now that you mention it, that's not such a bad idea," Griz says with a wink. "Lucky for you, that's what saddlebags are for."

"Good thinking. Take it easy, guys," I say, wrapping up my transaction and heading back to my car. I back out of the parking space, point the front-end toward the road and smash the gas, sending the rear-end into a barely-controlled fishtail. I back off the throttle, satisfied with my unnecessary display of horsepower.

A block further down the road I hear a rumble approaching. I look to my rearview mirror just in time to see RJ and Griz speed up to me then split apart, flanking me as I drive down the road. With RJ riding along the shoulder and Griz sitting right alongside me on the center line. He engages the clutch and rolls on the throttle. Even with the bike traveling at forty miles-per-hour, the exhaust still unleashes a thunderous roar. I look over at him through my window and nod. It's on.

He releases the clutch and we both slam our respective accelerators. He quickly pulls away because of the Harley's light weight and superior acceleration, merging into my lane in front of me. However, as we get closer to triple digits, my Cobra's top-end speed starts to come into play and I begin to reel him in. I pull out from behind him, shifting into the oncoming lane of traffic. As my front tires approach his back tire, I see a semi round a curve, headed directly for me. I jam on the brakes and slide back behind Griz as the semi passes by. My heart rate surpasses the RPMs of my engine instantly. Griz steals a glance back at me, raising his left arm from his handlebars and flips me off. What a dick.

I pull into my driveway and Griz is already there. RJ turns in behind me. I step inside the house and toss the pack of cigarettes to my dad who hadn't budged an inch since I left. Griz was plopping down in the recliner with the phone in his hand.

"Prospect, come to McGee's and get this beer before it gets warm," he instructs into the receiver. He hangs up without waiting for a response. That's the beauty of being a full-patch member in the MC. You bark some orders, no matter how ludicrous or inefficient, and the prospect has to jump. Griz turns his focus to me. "Rematch. Gimme a week and we'll make it an official race."

"Griz, you know you beat me here, right? When does the winner ever demand a rematch?"

"Chicken shit," dad chimes in from the couch. He shifts in his seat and a pistol falls to the floor. Cool. Real responsible, dad.

"I never said no," I point out. "Let's do it now." I push the point a little bit.

"Nah, I need a week," Griz answers. "I got some work to do on my bike."

"That's a load of shit. You suggested the race, now want some time to fix your bike up to make sure you beat me," I say.

He opens his mouth to respond when we hear somebody pull up to the house. We all glance out the picture window and see the prospect walking up. Riot Richards steps into the living room and greets the group. Club members tend to give each other nicknames, or road names, if you will. RJ is just his initials. Dad doesn't really have a formal road name as our surname just rolls off the tongue so well, so the MC simply calls him McGee. Griz originated from the burly stature of his typical biker appearance, looking like a grizzly bear. Riot, on the other hand, was so pre-disposed to a life of lawlessness that his parents saddled him with the natural-born name of Riot. That's not a nickname, no. It's his literal first name.

"Prospect, grab the beer from the bikes and take it to the clubhouse to keep it cold," Griz says. "I ain't trying to waste money on no skunk beer."

"Hold on," dad speaks up. "Griz, let's make this race a little more interesting." Griz and I both perk up. Riot pauses out of curiosity. "If Griz wins, the prospect gets patched in. If Will wins, we double the prospect period."

Griz and I have opposite reactions. He relishes the idea and laughs out loud at the proposed stakes. I shy away, failing to make the connection about how that wager is relevant to the race, other than the fact that Riot just happened to walk into the middle of the conversation. And I certainly don't want to be responsible for keeping him from being voted into the Kings.

"What do you think, VP? Think we can make that happen?" dad asks RJ. He's been sitting silently through this whole interaction and I think we all damn-near forgot he's still here.

"I think we can do that," he says with a smirk on his face.

Great.

Riot fires daggers at me from his gaze. I know, Riot. I know.

*****

I spend the week tuning up the Cobra, prepping it, and getting it dialed in for the impending contest. I skip school a couple days to make sure I have plenty of time to get the work done. Luckily, nobody watches over my shoulder insisting that I go to school, so that wasn't an issue. Maybe that should be unfortunately instead of luckily. Meh, who knows.

    I check in at Griz's Garage once or twice to see what he's up to. His bike is on the lift every time I stop by, with random parts removed and strewn about the work space. I notice a bottle that looks like an old-school oil tank, but his bike already has one of those so I'm confused about what it could be until I roll it over and spot three letters on the side: NOS. Holy shit, this hillbilly's gonna blow his ass up.

    I feel like I should also mention the other empty bottles laying around the bike. Mixing a bonus explosive liquid into a machine that is already designed to ignite another explosive liquid is ballsy. Doing so while under the influence is suicidal. Not that I would expect any different from these guys though.

    Race day rolls around and we meet up at the Kings' clubhouse. I step inside and see Riot tending to the bar. Normally, sixteen-year-old kids don't waltz into the clubhouse of an outlaw motorcycle club, but I wouldn't say I live a normal sixteen-year-old life.

Riot notices my presence and casts an icy stare in my direction. I spot RJ in the back, playing pool with the club's road captain, El Capitán, or El C for short. Dad is lounging on a couch smoking, but it doesn't appear to be one of the cigarettes I got for him the other day, if you catch my drift. Griz is sitting on a different couch with Stitch, another full-patch member. There's a credit card and rolled up bill, along with a small mirror on the coffee table in front of them. The mirror has lines of cocaine sorted out. I guess that's one way to get amped up for the race.

There's a set of closed doors along the far wall with the club's Skull King logo adorning them. Beyond that is the meeting room where the Kings conduct all their official business. A back hallway leads to a bathroom and a couple bedrooms where guys will crash after big parties, when they're otherwise too inebriated to ride home, to keep from actually crashing.

RJ looks up and sees me. "Will's here," he announces. "Race time." Everybody perks up and looks my way.

"Let's go!" Griz bellows, encouraging the crowd to move toward the door. He walks by me, punching me in the arm as he passes. He doesn't unload his full force on me, but it's still enough to make my opposite arm hurt. I do everything in my power to mask my reaction. I look him in the eye to show that he didn't shake me. Mind games. Posturing. Call it what you will, but the key is to show no weakness. I expect to earn a little respect, but all I notice is that his pupils are pegged from the stimulant he's been ingesting all morning. Great. That's a good sign before we operate some motor vehicles at high speeds in close proximity to one another.

We step outside to a roaring rumble as about a dozen Harley's fire up and are revved with excitement. The bikes roll out, lining the side of Clubhouse Road and blocking intersections to make sure Griz and I don't end up with any unwanted surprises as we tear down the street.

Griz mounts up on his bike and hits the ignition. The bike growls to life, sounding distinctly different than it has in the past. The engine sputters a time or two as Griz slowly rolls to the edge of the property, where the dead-end road becomes a small cul-de-sac style turnaround. Man, I hope he got the compression right for the upgrades he made this week.

I climb in the Cobra and start it up. I press on the gas a couple times because that seems to be the thing to do. The throaty exhaust note rips out of the straight pipes from under the rear bumper and the car tilts to the side slightly from the power of the engine twisting the frame and straining against the motor mounts under the hood. I idle up next to Griz and look over at him. We roll up onto the street and come to a stop with our front tires resting on the spray painted starting line.

One of the King's old ladies stands in front of us, a shop rag in her right hand. She raises her arm straight over her head and holds it there. She points at Griz with her left hand, yelling, "Are you ready?" He nods his head slightly to acknowledge her question. She then points to me. "Are you ready?" she asks again. I nod, affirming my response. She raises her left arm straight up to match her right arm and holds it there. I keep my left foot firmly on the brake while my right foot begins pressing against the gas pedal, sending the engine into a sustained rev, waiting for takeoff. I can barely hear Griz doing the same thing over the sound of my Mustang.

The flag drops and we both mash our accelerators. I see the front wheel of his bike come slightly off the ground as he launches from the starting line. My rear tires sling dirt and gravel, begging to find traction on the asphalt, before finally gaining purchase and sending me directly toward the finish line. Griz takes a quick and expected lead, just like last week. We speed past the observers, who are whooping and hollering along the side of the road, revving their engines, and generally just causing a ruckus. Zero-to-sixty comes and goes in no time. Another block into the race and we're approaching triple digits yet again. This is where I start feeling a little more confident, knowing that this road is just over a mile and a half, which means I have plenty of time to catch up and surpass him for the win, unlike our previous encounter.

This time though, as I begin to creep up alongside him, I notice the right thumb on this throttle hand stretch over to a new button attached to his handlebar. I get right next to him when the NOS sprays a mist into the engine and Griz's bike jolts forward, walking away from me as I approach my top speed. Dammit.

In a blink, it all goes sideways. I see Griz's motor blow apart as it happens. A rod is thrown through the engine casing followed by a small flash of an explosion, right up through Griz's legs, damn-near blowing his loins clean off and shredding the gas tank along the way. Gasoline and nitrous oxide flows from the obliterated engine and gas tank, soaking him and undoubtedly impairing his vision. He lowers his feet, dragging them atop the pavement as his bike slows and eventually rolls to a stop. I notice Griz flailing wildly, as his arms and chest are set aflame from being doused in explosive liquids. I blow by him at full speed about three hundred feet from the finish line, sentencing Riot to twice the length of a typical prospect period. The side of my car absorbs some shrapnel as I pass by, my driver-side window shattering from pieces of engine debris as the bike continues to vibrate and shutter a fast and violent death.

    Shit. Not really a good way to make friends within the club, but what're ya gonna do? It's not like I was going to back down from the race and look like a little punk, or purposefully throw the race just to spare Riot's feelings, and when my opponent couldn't even finish the race, my options were limited as to whether or not I was going to pull off the win.

I double back to check on Griz and make sure he's okay. There's already a crowd of Kings around him, patting out the fire before it has a chance to do any severe damage to Griz's exposed arms. Several of them shift their attention to me as I approach. They clap and congratulate me for winning the race.

Really? Your patch brother just about blew his hillbilly ass off and you want to congratulate me instead of checking on him? I seriously have to question the loyalty and devotion of these guys, questioning if I'm destined for this lifestyle.

There's a nearby mailbox blown open, either from the back draft of my blinding speed, or as a result of the miniature explosion that took place right in front of it. We'll probably never know which one it was for sure, but there's mail scattered along the ground that had fallen out of it. A pamphlet blows along the pavement, catching on my foot. I bend down to pick it up, intending to return it to the rightful recipient, but the message catches my attention.

Will you accept the challenge? It reads. The logo for the United States Air Force sits below it, with the picture of an Airman standing at full attention, saluting, next to it. The message comes across loud and clear, hitting me right between the eyes. **Will, accept the challenge.** I guess we'll see what happens from here. You know what they say - time will tell.

Learn more about the series:

Follow Will's journey as he flees Rough River Falls, only to be called back to the area in the Kings of Chaos Motorcycle Club Series. Think of that one biker show from California where the crow flies straight – yeah, that's the one – if it had a sense of humor and less murder.

Go along for the ride with Will as he finds his calling in life, then faces off with the demons from his past. His loyalty to lifelong friends and his hometown as a whole will be tested, as he tries to navigate his way through one tough decision after another. Not to mention all the repercussions from those decisions…

A Beast Forged
Written by: Christian Scully

I've lost track of time in here. It feels like decades since the war with Constantine ended. Since I was kidnapped and forced into this cell. Bill, my love, I miss you so much. The things I've had to endure in here...torture is too simple of a word to describe the level of Hell I have found myself in. They pit us against one another like gladiators fighting to the death for their entertainment. Not a week goes by without me either fighting for my life, being beaten until I'm motionless, or being raped. They force us to drink blood to enhance our abilities. Testing which abilities are the strongest. If it weren't for Vlad showing himself to me in my dreams, I'd have begged for death already. They claim it's all for the science of this disease. That we should feel privileged for our role in finding a cure to vampirism. Fuck that. We aren't fucking vampires. We're Infected. I hate to say it, but I sort of understand why Constantine went insane. Having these things done to me for who knows how long. I can understand his motivation for wanting revenge. I've given up on escaping this place. I'll see you soon, my love. I can't take much more of this. I love you, Bill.

    Erika opens her eyes. The single halogen bulb above her burns a blinding white. The numbing hum from it gives her a headache. The slate cell has just enough room for her bed, a sink with a mirror, and a toilet. She struggles to sit up. Her arms wrap around her stomach as her fingers clench on the orange jumpsuit in pain. *Fucking broken ribs,* Erika tells herself. She stares in the mirror. Her matted black hair hangs over her shoulders hiding the oval shape to her face. She rubs at the cracks and blisters over her thin lips. Her button nose is covered in scars and scratches.

"Breakfast!" A stern male voice shouts from outside her room. She glances at the steel door. A small slot opens near the bottom. The unknown guard tosses in a tray with yellow slop and a stale piece of bread. *Eggs...my favorite.* Erika stands to her feet only to collapse to the concrete floor. *What the Hell?* She complains, dragging herself towards the tray. She struggles towards the nearest wall and forces herself to sit with her back against it. Her forefinger and middle finger of her right hand reach out and pull the tray towards her. The door slams open tossing the tray across the room.

"What the fuck? Can't this bullshit wait until after breakfast?" Erika exclaims with anger. Three bulky guards dressed in black metallic suits stand over her. Their facemasks hide their identity. They lean over and pull her to her feet.

"Boss wants a chat." One of the guards replies. Erika glances between the three.

"Not sure which of you said that. Maybe

show me your face and we can come to some sort of agreement. Unless you're too much of a bitch," she snaps back. The guards drop her and swing at her with electrical batons. Erika curls into a ball. Her arms cover her head as she is beaten.

"Not another word, vamp." The same voice answers. They drag her out of the room. The hallway is the same drab gray as her room with a center row of halogen lights illuminating it. Men and women shout and scream at her. Erika fades in and out of consciousness. Her eyes close as her head drops in front of her.

Erika slowly regains consciousness. Blue walls surround her with white trim. A large mahogany desk sits in front of her. She glances down at her body. Her arms and legs are handcuffed to a wooden chair across from the desk. Blood covers the front of her jumpsuit.

"Great. And I just got this dry cleaned," Erika remarks with a half-hearted smirk.

"About time you woke up, Miss Lorenz. I

feared you had left us," a bellow replies from in front of her. Erika glares up at the thin framed man in front of her. He's tan with charcoal hair and a matching goatee. He wears a black dress shirt, navy blue tie, and a lab coat over it.

"Like I could get that lucky, Doctor Gomez." She spits blood to the floor. He casts a disgruntled glance at the stain before turning his powerful brown eyes at her.

"Miss Lorenz, it's come to my attention that some of the subjects…" he begins.

"Prisoners. The least you could do is call us what we are," she replies with distaste. He covers his mouth and coughs into his hand.

"Some of the *subjects* look up to you as some sort of hero. Do you know why?"

"Might have something to do with the fact I killed the guy you replaced."

"You're in no situation to make jokes, Miss Lorenz. I'm not as cordial as he was. Not with your kind." He glares into her brown eyes. The soft green rings around her irises flare out in a brilliant emerald coating the room in a glow. "That...is why. Right there. No other vampire has eyes that can do that. Where did you get them?"

"That whore you call a father," Erika retorts. The glow from her eyes fades.

"Don't! Just tell me who turned you. Now!"

"I was infected. Not turned. What is wrong with you humans. This isn't some magical sparkle dust bullshit. It's a fucking disease that none of you seem to understand."

"Then who *infected* you?" he demands. His glare pierces into Erika's eyes. *If I tell him, I'm as good as dead,* she thinks while biting her lower lip.

"I already told you, your mother." She smirks. He snaps his fingers angrily. A guard storms in and touches Erika's ribs with an electrical baton. She jerks in pain and screams out.

"I don't have the patience for your smartass attitude. You've made four attempts at escape and killed dozens of our guards. I was sent here to squelch any further revolt. Now, either you tell me who infected you or you can spend the night in The Pit." He stares her down intently. Erika glares at him.

"One of these days, I'm going to get loose again. When I do, I'm coming straight for you." Erika's eyes flare out briefly.

"Put her under The Blood Project. We're done here." He flicks his hand at her.

"NO! I won't drink! I refuse!" Erika struggles to free herself. The guard rushes over and smacks her across the forehead with the baton. She goes limp with pain.

"You don't have to drink. We have methods for forcing you to participate. I will find out your secret, Erika Lorenz. And I will find out why you are so important to so many vampires," he leans in and whispers at her. "Take her to the infirmary. Make her drink," he orders the guard. The handcuffs release their grip around her wrists. The pain in her head disorients her. The cuffs around her ankles release, but still she is unable to move. The guard lifts her petite frame over his shoulder and carries her out of the room. Erika stares down at the concrete floor as she is carried towards the infirmary.

"Erika Lorenz! The Hero of Shelton! We love you!" A distant voice shouts. Erika is too disoriented to tell who or where it is coming from.

"Help us!" Another voice shouts in response. *Don't pass out. Don't pass out. It'll make it too easy for them. Just keep conscious.* Erika struggles to keep her eyes open. *Erika, it's okay. You can rest. Let me handle this.* A male voice answers in her head. *No, Vlad. They must never know. They must never know the truth. It'll only make things worse.* She replies. *You'll die if you keep this rouse going. It's time to unleash who you really are. Bring fear to all that stand before you.* Vlad responds in desperation. *It won't work. I'm not like him. I'm not an heir. I'm not an Immortal. I'm nothing.* A tear falls to the concrete from her eyes. *You were infected by The Immortal, my heir. Let me protect you.* He pleads. *Just keep me conscious. Keep talking to me. I can do the rest.*

The guard storms into the infirmary and dumps her onto a metal table. The ceiling is lined with similar lighting to the hallway. The walls are lined with countertops that contain various medical devices. She notices a closed steel door through the gap in her feet. Erika struggles to regain control of her body. She reaches up at him with her right arm. The guard knocks her hand down with a pat of his own. He handcuffs her wrists and ankles to the table with little effort.

"Don't do this. You know what's going to happen, right?" Erika begs. His faceless mask stares back at her. "You know what happens in The Pit? You do this, you're responsible for what happens in there. Just like the rest of them." He turns away from her and grabs a plastic funnel.

"I'm sorry. I have no choice," he asserts.

"Y-Yes you do. Just leave. Let me escape. I won't tell anyone. I promise."

"You don't get it. There is no escaping this

place. We're a mile underground with biosensors at every door. You're a vamp. The sensors won't work for you. Not to mention what they would do to my little girl. Honestly, I'm sorry, but I can't risk my daughter for a vamp."

"Then show me your face," Erika begs. He steps back confused. "When I do escape...I want to know what the only survivor of this place looks like."

"Did you not hear me? There is no escape for you."

"Probably...but I don't want to accidentally leave your daughter without her father. Just show me your face. You've heard the stories about me. When I go into my blood rage, I don't want to attack you by accident," Erika pleads. He shakes his head in aggravation.

"Fine. But you're going to drink without me having to shove this damn funnel down your throat." He rips off his mask. His wavy blonde hair droops over his cheeks. His blue eyes glare into hers. His face is full and pale.

"Agreed. Thank you."

"Whatever. Why is it that important anyway? Vamps can't control themselves in a blood rage."

"Yeah, well, I can," she responds. He uncuffs her wrists. Erika forces herself to sit. He hands her a pouch of blood. "For brief moments. Like long enough to recognize a face." She struggles to open the pouch. He rips it from her weak grasp and opens it.

"You're getting too weak. Even if the stories about you are true. This could be your last time in there." He hands her the opened pouch. Erika leans her head back and drinks the scarlet contents until it is empty.

"Hurry, uncuff me and leave. It won't be long. Lock the door behind you," she tells him. He uncuffs her ankles and rushes for the door. He places the mask over his face and glances back at her. The room fills with a dark forest glow. She turns back at him. Her eyes are bloodshot and emanating a terror inducing gaze.

He races into the hallway and slams the door shut behind him. Erika flails wildly towards the door. Her fists slam into the steel. She growls and hisses. Foam pools over her lips. The door at the opposite end of the room squeals open. Erika rushes through the opening into the darkness.

    She rushes into a circular room with dim yellow lighting. Erika slides across the dirt floor hurling dust into the air. She feverishly inspects her surroundings. A spot light clanks on showcasing an executive suite near the top of the hundred-foot ceiling. Doctor Gomez stands at the large window with a bunch of men in suits surrounding him.

    "Miss Lorenz, it is time for your punishment," his voice echoes towards her. She growls in response. "Due to your lack of compliance, I decided it would be a great time to introduce you to our *other* champion." A large metal garage door rolls open. A bald behemoth of a man stands on the other side of the door.

His orange jumpsuit is torn into rags that expose most of his muscular figure. Only the area between his waist and knees is covered. His sky-blue eyes have iron colored rings that surround his pupils. He roars with anger and rushes her. Erika dodges to the side as he swipes down at her head. She kicks at his stomach. He catches her foot and tosses her against the concrete wall.

"Gentlemen. Tonight is a special fight. The So-Called Hero of Shelton faces off against The Giant. Bids start at fifteen thousand," Doctor Gomez tells the suits around him. A waiter in a suit and tie takes credit cards from all the men.

"Is she really as good as they say?" One of the business men asks.

"She is reported to have killed Constantine. Although there is no verification that he is dead. In here, she has been undefeated however," Doctor Gomez replies.

Erika weaves in between The Giant's clawing hands. She punches at his elbows. He backsteps and grabs her by the collarbone. He lifts her five-foot figure over his head and slams her to the ground. Blood spurts from her mouth. She wraps her legs around his arm and bites down on his knuckles. He screams in pain as blood rushes into her mouth. The Giant shakes his arm trying to free it from her grip. *Unleash me, now!* Vlad demands in her mind. Erika growls angrily in response. Her grip on The Giant's arm weakens. She is flung against the wall. The Giant roars with rage. Each stomp from his feet flings dust into the air blocking their view from one another. Erika grabs a handful of dirt and tosses it at his eyes. He stammers backwards and claws at his eyes in pain. Erika sprints toward him. She steps off his knee and flings her legs around his neck. She twists around his body to sit on his shoulders. Erika begins elbowing down on the top of his head.

"She sure is tenacious, but the size difference is just too much. There's no way she can win," another suit remarks about the fight.

"I don't know. If the stories are true...she killed thirty vamps with only daggers. That has to count for something," another replies.

"Maybe, but they don't have weapons in here. Plus, a Gray against a Green is not comparable. Super strength defeats cunning wit any day."

The Giant grabs Erika by the hair and rips her off his shoulders. He punches down at her chest. His brutal attack crushes her ribs. Blood flies from her mouth. Erika screams out in pain. The green glow in her eyes fades. He grabs her head and lifts her into the air. His fingers gripping into her temples. Erika struggles to free herself, to no avail. The Giant storms towards the concrete wall and slams her head against it repeatedly. She continues to struggle against him. Moments later, her body goes limp. The Giant continues to slam her against the wall. Her face is bloodied and broken. He turns her towards him and licks the blood clean from the remains of her face. He drops her body and storms out of the ring.

"There you have it. The Giant is the victor," Doctor Gomez announces with excitement. The suits are ablaze with mixed emotions. Doctor Gomez snaps his fingers. The waiter rushes to his side. "Have her corpse taken to the incinerator immediately. She gets no burial." The waiter nods and exits the suite.

"You knew that was going to happen!" one of the business men shouts at Doctor Gomez.

"I had my suspicions, but she has proven herself formidable before. There was always a chance she could have beaten him. You would have been a fool to not think so and I do not do business with fools," he tells the suit before walking out of the executive suite. Two guards march in-step with him. "Let's break the news to the *subjects*," he informs the guards. They nod in silent response. They make their way towards the holding cells. The hall is lined with orange suited inmates with various colored rings in their eyes. Each has a guard gripping at the back of their collar. Doctor Gomez smiles at the crowd.

"Fuck you, Doc!" a male voice shouts from the crowd.

"And good morning to you too. I called you all out here to inform you that your beloved Hero of Shelton has *fortunately* passed away. Let her death be a warning for you all. I will not stand for *any* further defiance!" He glares into the crowd. "You will all comply with orders as directed from here on out or you will meet her same fate. And to squelch any hopes of memorial...her body is currently on its way to the incinerator," Doctor Gomez shouts over the inmates screams and gasps. "Put the *animals* back into their cages," he says, spit flying from his mouth. The guards nod in silent response before returning the crying inmates to their cells. Doctor Gomez heads down the hall to his office.

Gomez opens the door to his office. The lights have been turned off coating the room in darkness. He peers inside and recognizes a large male figure sitting in the metal chair across from his desk. The figure sits motionless. The doctor sighs before flicking on the lights and entering the room. The mysterious man has broad shoulders and a shaved, pale head. He wears a black leather jacket over a gray tee and worn jeans. Black combat boots complete his outfit. Doctor Gomez closes the door behind him.

"You're back," the man states sternly. Doctor Gomez marches to his brown leather chair and sits without a word. "Do you have any new information for me?" the figure asks. The man has a bulky, rounded face. His brown irises are surrounded with orange rings.

"Not anything related to your needs, no. I thought you had been killed?"

"You do remember our agreement, right?"

"Of course, Constantine. You've made it blatantly obvious that you're looking for an Immortal. It'll just come when *I* decide it. Not you. This facility runs because I say it does and you need us," Doctor Gomez replies in a threatening tone. Constantine slowly rises to his feet. His eyes fixed on the doctor. In a flash, he reaches across the table and yanks Doctor Gomez within inches of himself. The guard preps his electrical baton and steps towards Constantine. Doctor Gomez waves at the guard to stop him.

"This *facility* runs because I want it to. You sit here because *I* allow it! You and your dogs are alive because *I* allow it!" Constantine growls.

"I...I...I may not have anything new about the Immortals, but I do have other information you might be interested in."

"Speak!"

"Erika Lorenz has been killed," Doctor Gomez trembles to say. Constantine's eyes widen with shock as he shoves the doctor back across the table.

"S-She...you're positive?"

"Yes. The Giant caved her head in. She's currently down at the incinerator. It should be over soon. We even have her daggers. Soon, there will be nobody standing in your way anymore."

"Make sure she is dead. That woman tends to play possum."

"I watched as her skull broke. No one could have survived that."

"Doctor, you have no idea what you have gotten yourself into by bringing her here. If what you say is true, call me when it's all done," Constantine stammers. He strides towards the door. The guard steps in front of him. The electrical rod at his side sizzles. "Move, or I'll make a meal of you," Constantine orders. The guard reluctantly steps to the side. Constantine storms out of the room. Doctor Gomez flicks his wrist at the guard, who follows Constantine out of the room.

"Damnit!" Doctor Gomez shouts, slamming his fists on the table. Papers scatter across the room. He grabs the phone and dials the incineration room number. "Is she gone yet?"

The incineration room is a bland concrete square. The only light comes from the mouth of a massive steel chamber. Erika's naked, lifeless body sits on a stainless-steel slab. A blood soaked, charcoal, long sleeve tee sits on top of ripped black skinny jeans and black work boots. On the opposite side of her body rests two ornate daggers. The blades are swirls of Damascus Steel. The hilts are wrapped in black leather with gold inlays depicting flying owls. Rubies cap the golden pummels at the end. A short, stout man stands in the dark holding a phone to his ear. His greasy red hair is pulled back into a ponytail.

"Not quite yet. She has just been prepped, sir," he replies.

"Get it done quick or you'll go in there, Frank!" Doctor Gomez demands over the phone. Frank nods in silent response before hanging up the phone. The room flashes with scarlet and emerald briefly. Frank blinks to regain his vision.

"What the Hell was that?" he mutters. He turns his attention to the table. Erika is nowhere to be seen. "W-What?" A small hand grabs his ponytail and tosses him against the concrete wall. A gasp of breath escapes him. Erika stands in front of him. Her eyes burning a forest green. She grabs his forehead and leans his head back.

"Fresh blood," Erika growls. The side of her left hand chops Frank's throat and crushes it against the wall. She turns toward the table. "Oh, how I have missed you," she tells the daggers. Erika grabs her clothes and gets dressed. Holes cover the bloodied shirt. *How did I survive this? How did I survive...now?* She asks herself. She sheathes the daggers against the small of her back. *You've become more. This place...you're immortal now.* Vlad replies. "How the Hell did I become immortal?" Erika asks. *Everything you have endured here. Every time you refused to let me take over. You're body went into survival mode. Fortunately for you, Bill infected you. Survival for you means his ability took over. To what extent, I'm not sure.* Vlad explains. "Okay then, let's do this." Erika unlocks the door and opens it. Four guards stand outside. They turn and jump back in surprise at her. Each one flicks open a baton that surges with electricity.

Erika sprints at them while sliding the daggers from behind her back. Her left hand spins the dagger so the blade rests against her forearm. The guards swing wildly at her. Erika weaves in and out of the attacks. She slices her left arm out at the throat of a guard while plunging her right into the chest of another. The weight of the guard falling pulls her airborne. Her feet connect with the wrists of the other two guards. Their batons fly down the hall. Erika yanks her dagger free. Blood sprays against the wall.

"I swear that was just luck," Erika smirks. She tosses the two daggers at the guards. The blades slide through the ceramic helmets and kill them instantly. A cacophony of stomping feet flood through the hall. "This can't be good," Erika remarks while tugging at the daggers to free them. She glances up just as fifty guards drown the hallway in a cloak of black armor. Each one holds a rifle aimed at her.

"Breach!" one of the guards shouts. Erika rushes back inside the incineration room just as bullets whiz past her head. She slams the steel door closed and kneels with her back against the concrete wall. *You got this. You've done this before. You can handle a few guards.* Bullets tear through the door with ease. *Granted...not against rifles like this.* A guard kicks the door open. Erika instinctively strikes a dagger through his thigh. She uses his body as a temporary shield while she rushes into the crowd. Bullets smack into his back as he screams and gargles in pain before dying. Erika tugs her dagger free and slices wildly at the crowd. Blood spurts from three guards as they collapse. *You can't do this by yourself. Let me take over.* Vlad begs. *Fine, but only this once.* Her eyes darken to an eerie black color. Her head drops. The guards back away from her with their rifles aimed at her chest.

"Finally." Erika's voice bellows in an eerie

tone. She lifts her head revealing her blackened eyes. An evil smirk crosses her lips. She spins the daggers into the beltline at the small of her back in a single fluid motion. The guards fire. Bullets pierce Erika's chest and abdomen causing her to rapidly spaz from left to right. The wounds heal instantly. The guards stop firing and attempt to flee. Erika grabs the nearest one and bites through the armor protecting his neck. Blood rushes into her mouth. She drops the lifeless body and lets out a primal scream. She pounces onto another and bites down. Plastic and metal fly through the hall. Screams and shouts of pain echo out as she tears through the guards one by one. She tears through all fifty within minutes. The walls are coated in blood. Sirens blare through the entire complex. Small turrets drop from the ceiling and aim at Erika. Tranquilizer darts fire out of the turrets and connect all over her body. Erika's black eyes fade to a soft lime. She pulls out the darts and takes in her blood-soaked surroundings.

"W-What?" Doctor Gomez asks terrified. Erika returns a furious gaze into his eyes. An emerald glow fills the hall. She reaches behind her back and slides out her daggers. *He's mine.* She tells Vlad. Doctor Gomez rushes behind the corner of the perpendicular hallway. Erika sprints after him. She turns the corner into a foot connecting with her forehead. The kick tosses her end over end down the hall.

"Rematch?" Erika smirks while climbing to her feet. Blood drips from her lips and a small cut on her nose. The Giant stomps toward her and roars. Erika stares into his bloodshot eyes. "You fed. Good. This might get interesting then."

The Giant swipes wildly at her. Erika slashes her daggers at his right elbow and wrist. A snap and whip sound reverberates through his body as his tendons rip into pieces. He falls to his knees holding his arm in pain while screaming. Erika kicks his chin upward before leaping in front of him. He lowers his head. Cold steel tinges his throat. He growls in submissive defiance.

"You aren't my enemy. I know how they use you. Give up and you live," Erika demands.

"They'll kill me," he growls. Erika slowly removes one of her blades from his throat and slices across her forearm. The Giant watches as the wound heals and leaves only a thin line of blood.

"I'm Immortal," Erika declares. The Giant nods slowly. "Good. Now, stay here and I'll get you help." She pulls her other dagger back and stands. Erika scans her options in the hallway. The Giant uses his left hand to point down the hallway he came from. Erika grabs both daggers in her right hand and pats his shoulder with her left. She jogs down the hall. The hall leads around another corner. She stops just before the turn and places her back against the wall. She glances around the corner briefly. *It's empty,* she realizes. She spins around the corner to doors lining both walls of the hall. *Great.* Erika grabs the nearest door handle. Heavy footsteps echo toward her from in front and behind. She readies her daggers and backs herself up against the wall to her right. *Keep my back here and they can't get behind me. As long as I can see them, I can make it out of this,* she tells herself. A horde of forty guards rush in carrying batons and body length fiberglass shields. The hall fills with the echo of cackling electricity from the batons. Doctor Gomez emerges from the mob.

"Miss Lorenz, you're outnumbered and outmatched. With such little space to maneuver, your particular ability is useless. Get back into your cage," he tells her. Erika stands and faces him. Her daggers spin back and forth in her hands.

"Not this time." Erika smirks. She flicks a dagger at Doctor Gomez. He dodges. The blade slices through the facemask of a guard standing behind him. The guards rush toward her. Erika jumps in the air and uses both of her feet to kick at a nearby shield. The wearer pushes back to keep from falling. The push sends Erika cascading through the air over the swarming guards behind her. *That was...way easier than I thought it would be.* Erika glances down at her remaining dagger. *Shit, I need to get the other one back.* She sprints toward the unorganized and confused mass. She slides under the legs of five guards, slicing the backs of their knees with her dagger. Batons swing down at her prone position. Erika grabs the leg of one of the incapacitated guards. Electricity surges through his body as each baton smacks into his leg. Erika rolls out from her protective shield and slices wildly into the crowd. She stands as her dagger shreds through the fabric of the armor and blood cascades from the stomachs of three guards. She stabs another guard in the stomach and uses the dead weight as a shield against further attacks from the batons. A sting surges through her left shoulder as a baton pummels into it. She spots her other dagger still imbedded in the face protector of the dead guard. Erika shoves the dead body free from her blade. Three guards swing down at her. She rolls toward her first victim and unsheathes it from the bloody holster of the guard's face. Doctor Gomez forces a jumbled path to free himself of the carnage. Erika casts the surrounding group an intimidating smirk. They close in around her from all sides. *You're an Immortal now. Let go of all inhibitions and let the beast within you free.* Vlad tells her. Erika closes her eyes. Her fingers partially release their grip on the daggers causing them to tilt downward in her subtle grasp. *Let your body numb. Feel nothing. Only then can you show them your power.* Erika's head drops as she collapses to a sitting position on the floor. The guards reluctantly close in around her. Each keeping their focus on her motionless body.

    Doctor Gomez returns with a pistol in hand. He aims it at her head and fires. The thunder deafens the hall. Guards grab painfully at their ears and bounce off each other's shoulders restricting Doctor Gomez's vision. A forest green glow fills the hall. Erika stands amongst the chaos. A guard holds a shield to cover himself. She stabs her dagger through it and into his chest, shattering the shield into pieces. Fiberglass chunks stick out of her arm. Erika's gaze is set on Doctor Gomez. The guards rush her. She swipes her daggers up and slices through the chests of two guards. She swings outwards and catches the temples of two more. She spins and flings the dead bodies into the crowd. A guard grabs her hair. She stabs back into his stomach before twisting around and rapidly stabbing his chest with both daggers. A baton smacks against the back of her head. She turns while throwing a dagger into another guard. Her free hand reaches out and grabs the attacker by the collar. Her fingers clench into his clothing. She pulls him towards her and headbutts him before stabbing through his chin.

"What the Hell is she?" a guard asks terrified.

"She's defiant. Take her down!" Doctor Gomez replies. He shoves five guards toward her. Erika glares into his eyes. She swipes her daggers at the guards. Their necks rip open, spraying blood across the walls. Her slow strides towards him cause the remaining seventeen guards to stumble and climb over one another trying to escape from Erika's wrath. She stabs her daggers down into the gaggle of bodies. Two more victims collapse to the floor. Three stand and try to climb over the drove of fear-riddled guards. Erika swipes her daggers from left to right in unison. Three heads spill over the bodies. Screams and shouts echo through the complex. Doctor Gomez steps backwards. He hugs the wall with his back. His eyes wide with fear.

"Twelve." Erika mocks. The horde get to their feet. Erika tosses her dagger at the guard in front of the group. It slides into his back causing him to collapse to the ground. She grabs the guard nearest her and drives her blade into his spine. A twist of her wrist causes him to go limp and motionless. The body drops. "Ten." The others rush to grab their shields in panic. She continues her march towards Doctor Gomez. Stepping in between bodies, she twists her hips from side to side. "Doc, how long do you think it'll take me to kill your last ten guards? Think you have time to run?" Erika smirks.

"W-What are you?" Doctor Gomez replies in terror. The remaining ten guards sprint out of sight.

"I'm what you created. Judgment incarnate," she replies calmly strolling towards the guard with her dagger in his back. She plucks it from its bloody sheath. With her back turned to him, Doctor Gomez attempts to escape. A dagger slams into the concrete at his feet. "You asked me who infected me. Bill Draig did."

"T-The Immortal?" His voice trembles. Erika smirks and nods in response. The hair on his arms and the back of his neck stand on end. "Y-You're an Immortal?"

"Thanks to you, Doc." Erika marches

towards him. A growing racket of footsteps fills the hall. "More of yours ready to die?"

"I. Please. Have mercy, please," he begs. Erika glances behind her. Her fellow prisoners file in. They stand in wait. "W-What? H-How?"

"She lives!" The crowd cheers. The Giant stands behind the crowd. Their heads only managing to reach his chest. Erika casts him a soft smile. He smirks and nods while grabbing his limp arm.

"Get them out of here and to Laura. I have unfinished business with the Doc," Erika demands. The congregation turn and march out of sight. Erika returns a rage filled glare toward Doctor Gomez. "How many of us did you kill for sport? How many died so you could make some quick cash? How *dare* you ask for mercy. Killing you here and now...that's too good for you." She turns and steps down the hall.

"Thank G-," Doctor Gomez begins. A dagger digs into his side causing him to collapse in pain.

"Then again...you made me a blood addict and I need a fix." Erika smirks. She rushes him. Her knee connects with his forehead causing his head to snap back against the concrete wall. She yanks his head to the side and bites into his shoulder. Her pupils dilate as blood rushes into her mouth. Minutes later she strolls toward the exit with Doctor Gomez's right hand clutched in hers. She reaches the door and places the bloody hand on the fingerprint sensor. The doors open. *Finally. Time to go home.*

Learn more about the series:

In the city of Shelton, Oregon, vampires aren't just a myth. They're a reality. An outbreak of a man-made virus, the Vorcino Virus, turned a significant portion of the population into creatures of the night. Each with their own special abilities and powers. *The Chronicles of Erika Lorenz* follows the journey of a normal college student with a questionable night job as she transforms from a damsel in distress into a war hero and a savior. Everything changes for Erika the night she is attacked by one of these bloodthirsty creatures. After almost becoming a meal, she finds herself trapped in a war between two vampire clans. One wants revenge on all of humanity for years of torture and senseless killing of the vampires. The other is trying a more diplomatic approach. The series focuses on Erika's internal struggles as she has to overcome the hurdles of those closest to her dying, being captured, becoming a vampire herself, and the other pains brought on by war. *The Chronicles of Erika Lorenz* is a three-part series with the first two novels currently available.

Arcadis Meets NoKon
Written by: George Kramer

NoKon was in enormous peril. He was bleeding bright red resin, and he was leaving a trail. Humans were trying to capture him, but he could not let that happen!

They had tracked him from his lair in Assuwa, or from what little intel he had gathered, Asia. He had not come out in centuries because of his need to slumber. Unusual sounds awakened him, and when he went to investigate, he had found human settlements. The nasty critters abounded all over his domicile.

After his awakening, he remembered something. It was a dream that foretold the end of all realities, and the magical being responsible lived far away in a different country in a remote area. He had to get to the person before it was too late.

He kept a discreet distance as he did not want any interaction. Unfortunately, they spotted him before he was able to disguise himself as one of them. He flew above the clouds so he would not be seen. Because of the distance involved, at nighttime, he assumed their form and fled Asia in a ship and landed in Southern Africa. Later on, NoKon made himself appear as a resident of a small village.

While there, he had learned a lot about the modern world, and he was not happy. His species were decimated to the point of extinction. He was now the tale of legends, the last of his kind.

His hunger was constant. He needed to consume something soon, or he would perish. The animal known as a camel were far and few between this far south. He traveled northwest to Morroco, where he feasted upon camels until he was caught in his natural form. And still, he was far from where he needed to be.

NoKon fled in another ship as a stowaway, and this time he landed in North America. His travels led him to Pennsylvania, where he gobbled up deer, bobcats, and black bears. Full strength returned to him after he consumed the bear. His confidence swelled. He was sure he could fly to his destination. However, his belief in his power was a mistake. Despite being in the modern world, NoKon decided it was time to show his pure form. After all, what could the humans do? At this point, arrows would bounce off him.

When he shifted his form, the people panicked. Their weaponry had advanced beyond his belief!

A few projectiles slammed into him while in midflight. He thought it wouldn't hurt him, but they went clear through his tough exterior. He landed on his right side while the humans slowly circled him. He turned into human form and noticed his right arm was shattered and bleeding. Managing to evade capture was difficult with his trail of bright red resin.

Somehow luck was on his side. He stayed clear of the main highways and remained in the woods. But the humans were persistent. Desperation and constant hunger made him careless as he feasted upon the animals which roamed the woodlands he navigated.

The dead carcasses and his resin made him an easy target. Not to mention, it was getting more challenging to shift forms.

NoKon's magic empowered him to communicate with other species, which helped him when he saw a black bear surround an old bobcat. NoKon knew the bear only wanted food to sustain itself, but the bobcat was old and defenseless. He succeeded in scaring the bear away. For his reward, NoKon asked if the bobcat could help him locate someone magical that would be able to save reality if it were in danger. The bobcat knew of a sorcerer that lived in Indiana who might be able to help. It seemed logical it was the same being from his dream.

His magic enabled him to read different languages too. He saw a sign for Knightstown, Indiana, so he knew he wasn't far from his goal of McCordsville. However, his bulky frame and his cumbersome ability to traverse the dwindling supply of wooded areas made his progress slow.

As the night approached and the temperature dipped, NoKon had to decide whether to continue his journey and risk exposure, or lay down, risk a different kind of exposure, and perish. When he was able to transform into a human, it was easy to find shelter.

He heard the rustling of leaves and tree branches moving. He was too tired to go on. Let the humans kill him, put him on display, and be proud of their accomplishment. Many species were extinct because of them, why not himself? As for the dream that foretold a sorcerer who could destroy realities? It would die with him.

NoKon would die with dignity. He would

look at his enemies in their puny eyes. He had no power left to protect himself or to cause them harm. Let them come.

NoKon counted four humans with camouflage gear. Each had a shotgun and was pointing at his broad forehead. He could do nothing but watch his demise unfold.

"There you are, you nasty critter! We've been hunting you from the outskirts of Scranton, Pennsylvania," the man with the long black beard stated.

He spit something out of his mouth that was thick and black. NoKon had no idea what the substance was.

Another man with a bright orange shirt said, "Yes sir, hoss! What we have here is truly a spectacle!"

"How much do you think we'll fetch for him?" one of the other men asked.

"I bet a pretty penny if he's alive, much less if he's dead."

"Well, we ain't keeping him alive! I reckon

he'll destroy our way of life, boys."

"Well, there you have it," the man with the long beard said. "We need to kill it and take it to the authorities."

"Why do we have to take it to the authorities, Chad?"

The man with the beard said, "What else do you want to do with it, Jeremiah?"

Jeremiah looked to his left and then to his right. "I say we eat it," he whispered to his friends.

"Eat it?" Chad said with repulsion.

"Yeah! He's so big we could split him four ways and still have meat for the next two years!"

The four men looked at each other.

"I don't know, Jeremiah..."

"C'mon Chad! How many people can say they had dragon meat?"

One of the men kicked NoKon and pointed. "But what about the scales? They're hard as a rock!"

Chad took out a long serrated knife. "This

will cut through anything." He sliced off one of the scales as NoKon roared in pain. Chad raised the knife above his head. "This will make a great trophy!"

The men nodded in agreement.

"Okay, boys, let's kill us a dragon!" Chad said with delight.

"I don't think so!"

Chad put down his knife, and the four men put up their shotguns.

"Did you say that, dragon?" Jeremiah asked as he aimed his shotgun at NoKon.

"Shoot that dragon, and you'll suffer the consequences," the invisible voice said.

Jeremiah moved his gun in the direction of the voice and fired.

"Stupid humans," the voice said as a purple bolt of energy erupted and blasted Jeremiah. Jeremiah was lifted from the magical power and flew into a nearby tree. He fell to the ground and shook his head in confusion.

"I don't know who you think you are, but

this here dragon is ours! We shot him first, and we aim to eat him!" Chad said as he spit out tobacco.

"Not on my watch," the invisible voice retorted. Purple energy blasts cascaded from nowhere and everywhere. The men were incapacitated within seconds. After several more seconds, the men got up and put up their hands in surrender.

A soft laugh came through the void. "You track an extremely rare magical being through a couple of states, planned on killing *and then eating him,* and now you think you can surrender as if nothing was wrong?"

"Yeah," Chad said. "It's the law. You can't do anything. We surrendered!"

"Human law, perhaps. Magical law? I don't think so."

"There's no such thing as magic. That's plain stupid!" Jeremiah spat.

"Yet, there lies a dragon, you stupid human."

"What do you plan on doing with us?" Chad asked with sudden fear.

A man appeared out of thin air. He was of average build, had messy brown hair, and had glasses. He wore a purple trench coat.

"My name is Jackson, and I am a Regulator for this section of Indiana."

Chad looked at the other men and shrugged. "What's a Regulator?"

"Humans call them policemen, and what am I going to do with you? Well, let me think. The best course of action would be to eradicate your existence, but the Convocation would have my head."

NoKon could not believe other magical beings existed besides him. There were rumors of other magical races, but they were folklore in his world. He paid close attention to the purple powered person.

"I am going to make you forget you ever laid eyes on the dragon and send you back to Pennsylvania," Jackson stated.

"You have no right, magician!" Chad yelled.

A second later, Jackson was inches from Chad's face. "Give me a reason to kill you so I can justify it to the Convocation!"

Chad remained quiet even though he did not know what a Convocation was.

"You have two choices, humans, and I care not the consequences of my actions. Either die or forget. What will it be?"

"We choose to die, magician!" Chad yelled as he ran to retrieve his shotgun.

Before he had the chance to pick the gun up, Jackson waved his hand, and the shotgun disappeared. He whispered an incantation which brought the four men in front of him and unable to move. Jackson encased them in a glowing purple bubble.

"Forget ever encountering the dragon, return from whence you came, and start reading more books," Jackson murmured.

Jackson waited until the purple bubble

disappeared before checking on the dragon.

"Do you speak the magic tongue or English?"

"I speak both."

"Good. Do you have a name, dragon?"

"NoKon."

Jackson nodded before resuming. "Up until today, dragons did not exist in this realm. Several centuries ago, they were killed off."

"I was slumbering for a long time. I woke up due to the human activity nearby. They saw me, chased me until I got to this country. The humans chased me from the east to here."

"Okay. Why are you here in Indiana? It can't be for sightseeing."

"In Pennsylvania, I was told of a legendary sorcerer that could help me."

"What can sorcerers do for you, NoKon?"

"I had a dream that foretold the end of the realities, and I think the sorcerer in question can help me here in Indiana. Does he or she have a name?"

"I think you're referring to Arcadis. He is the most powerful red primary powered sorcerer in the known realms.

"Red primary power?"

"Yes, the primary rulers of the universes are the three primary colors; red, blue, and yellow."

"But, you're purple. Where do you fit in?"

"I am a secondary, an offspring resulting from a red primary and a blue primary powered sorcerer."

"Why is Arcadis the most powerful of all if there are three primary colors?"

"Because he has Lord Quill's power infused inside him."

"Is red the most powerful color, Jackson?" NoKon asked quietly.

"Yes."

"Why?"

"Because red represents anger which fits most of the red powered sorcerers. Blue is next because that represents passion. Yellow is the least powerful because it represents happiness, which makes them the last ones that want to engage in battle."

NoKon closed his eyes and gradually opened them. His breath became difficult. "I fear I am dying. I want to thank you for saving me. Do you possess the necessary power to transport me to Arcadis?"

"Yes, but first, you need to be mended magically, and that requires going to the Convocation. However, be warned. There is growing tension between the primaries and the secondaries, which may result in an inevitable war."

"I am only concerned with speaking with Arcadis. Your war is your war, and I will not get involved. You have my word."

"Dragon's word is their bond. I will do as you ask."

Jackson created a large magical elevator to accommodate the dragon's size. Jackon magically lifted NoKon inside and disappeared.

*****

They emerged in the hallway of the Convocation, causing an immediate uproar. Sorcerers of every color came to the dragon that shouldn't exist.

"What is the meaning of this, Jackson?" demanded Madame Gildeon.

Jackson gave a deep bow. "Madame, this is NoKon, the last of the dragons. He awoke from a long sleep. He had a dream that foretold an event. He is severely injured, but wishes to speak to Arcadis."

"NoKon, I am the leader of the Convocation and Arcadis's mother. Arcadis isn't on our realm. He is… on earth at his antique store when he should be attending to more important matters *here*."

"Madame, I must speak with your son," NoKon whispered.

"I will decide if you get to speak with him,"

Madame Gildeon quipped.

"Madame, with all due respect, please hear him out," Jackson replied with downcast eyes.

"Are you telling me how to conduct my business, Regulator?"

"No, Madame. I only request your indulgence."

Despite NoKon's condition, he was able to discern the tension between the exchange. He saw the tension between Jackson's faction and Madame Gildeon's faction. There will be a war, that much NoKon knew.

"First, he needs magical medical attention, and he is too large for the infirmary. I doubt the infirmary is equipped to handle his physiology," Madame Gildeon said as if she were thinking out loud.

After a few minutes of careful thought, Madame Gildeon said, "Okay, I will need all of the primaries to help me mend the dragon."

"What about the secondary's help?"

Jackson asked with measured anger.

"You don't possess the necessary power, Jackson."

"What? I stopped the humans from killing him, I transported him, and I have the necessary power to help you!"

"You dare question me?"

"Yes, Madame Gildeon, I do!"

Jackson snapped his fingers. Several hundred secondaries lined up beside him, and several dozen primaries lined up beside Madame Gildeon.

"I am sick and tired of being treated like a second-hand magical being!"

"You dare to use magic in the sacred halls of the Convocation?" Madame Gildeon bellowed.

"Yes!" Jackson hurled a purple-powered blast at her. She put up a shield the second before the purple energy hit her.

"That tickled," Madame Gildeon said with torment in her voice.

She shot Jackson with a potent red

primary blast. It hit Jackson squarely in his chest. Despite having a force field up, he was pushed back and slammed into his army of secondaries.

War was now imminent.

*****

Arcadis was selling used comic books to a man and his son in McCordsville, Indiana, at his antique store when he felt a tremor in the magical world. As soon as they left, Arcadis knew he had to go to the Convocation immediately.

*****

Arcadis appeared in the middle of a maelstrom. He put up a shield and dispersed a full blast of red primary magic in every direction.

"Enough!" he thundered. His command reverberated across the expanse of the vast hall.

Almost three-quarters of the purple,

green, and orange secondaries were thrown to the floor from his blast, and a quarter of the primaries were down.

"Two questions! What is the meaning of this conflict, and what the hell is a supposedly extinct dragon doing in the hallways of the Convocation?"

"Sire, if I may?" asked Jackson.

"No, you may not!" Arcadis thundered back.

"Let him speak," NoKon said as loud as he could muster.

"Excuse me, dragon? You have no say in this matter," Arcadis said with anger.

"On the contrary, I do. If all of you would shut up for a minute, Jackson can explain."

"How dare you!" Madame Gildeon spat.

"Madame, if I were at full power, I would roast you where you stand for your lack of respect. Now, be quiet and hear him out!"

"That does it!" Madame Gildeon was powering herself up when NoKon, with great difficulty, rose.

"You kill me, and you will have to answer to a higher power!"

"I answer to no one!"

Arcadis wedged himself between his mother and NoKon.

"Mother, please stand down. I need to know what is going on. Dragon, what is it that you seek?"

"How dare you interrupt me, Arcadis! I am your mother and leader of the Convocation!"

Arcadis gave such a deep bow that his red trench coat hit the floor. "Mother, I apologize. But I need to hear what the dragon has to say because it concerns me. Please allow me to hear him out."

"I will allow it, son. Continue dragon."

"I am too weak to explain. Jackson will explain."

Arcadis turned to Jackson. "Now that I have my mother's permission… speak."

Jackson recounted what had transpired.

After he was finished, the room became silent.

"NoKon, what was your dream that seems to involve me?" Arcadis asked with concern.

"I dreamt, a couple of years from now, you do something so horrific that it demands *Deus's* attention. After that? You seek to recreate reality by employing an extremely potent spell that goes awry that leaves the multiverse in shambles."

"What? That's impossible! Even I don't have that kind of magical power."

"Oh, but you will, Arcadis."

"You see, secondaries? In the future, Arcadis, a primary mind you, ends up screwing up not only our reality, plus all of the others!" Jackson lamented.

"That's only one possible future which is never written in stone, Jackson!" Arcadis retorted.

"No, my dreams are never wrong, Arcadis. It will happen!" NoKon said with assurance.

"Then to rectify the situation, Arcadis must die!" yelled Jackson as he threw a purple blast at an unsuspecting Arcadis. He flew into several primaries.

When he came back to Jackson, Arcadis's eyes were red, and the pentagram on his chest burned a hole in his shirt, exposing glowing red primary power.

"Now you will feel my wrath, Jackson!"

The war that Jackson had told NoKon earlier was now in full swing.

As Arcadis unleashed his mighty power, thunder rattled the vast hallway. Lightning followed. Several of the lightning strikes hit statues and shattered them. The rumbling increased to such a crescendo that the fighting momentarily stopped.

Soon a figure of pure energy appeared before them.

"Who are you?" demanded Arcadis.

"I am *Divinius!*"

"Who?" asked Arcadis.

"I am the first son of *Deus*!"

"Impossible. That title goes to a human

being from two thousand years ago."

Divinius put up an energy hand and zapped Arcadis. "Fool! I have been around for billions and billions of years!"

Arcadis was unprepared for the magnitude of his power. He was propelled nearly forty-five feet and taking sorcerers along the way. When he was able to get up, he sauntered to *Divinius*.

"So, your power is formidable. What of it?"

"You don't understand what is going on here, do you Arcadis? You never have," *Divinius* said with disgust.

"That's because we've never met!"

"And that is precisely why I am here!"

"What does that even mean?" Arcadis asked in confusion.

Divinius turned to NoKon. "You don't belong here, dragon."

"Why? He was telling me some interesting things about my future."

"A future you're not supposed to know

about until the time it occurs."

"I woke up from a dream and was compelled to tell Arcadis," NoKon said with reverence.

"You dragon, are an anomaly. You should not exist in this reality. All those things you spoke about are actions that have not occurred yet. I will not allow you to say anything further!"

"But now that you know them, why can't you stop them from happening *now*?" Arcadis asked.

"*Deus* allows me to see things, and then he doesn't. I do as I am told," *Divinius* said as he looked at NoKon.

"So this war between the primaries and secondaries, me doing something horrific that angers *Deus*, my spell that recreates reality, and its impending doom will happen?" Arcadis asked in astonishment.

The outline of *Divinius* tilted upward. "I am allowed to answer you. Yes, it will occur in a couple of years from now."

"And now you too will erase our memories?" Arcadis asked with concern.

"I must. It is *his* command that I do so."

"In the future, how do I attain so much magical power?"

"I am unable to answer that question, Arcadis. You must live out your life until such time when the circumstances present themselves." *Divinius* turned to NoKon. "You first. I know not why you are here, or why you had that dream, but I cannot allow your existence in my realms."

NoKon bowed. "I understand."

Divinius raised a hand made of pure energy.

"Can we at least talk about this, *Divinius*?" asked Arcadis.

"No, and don't do anything stupid Arcadis! I know you too well!"

Divinius snapped his fingers, and NoKon was gone. He faced the horde of sorcerers.

"I want to keep my memory of this event.

Please!" Arcadis implored.

"No. In the future, you will upset the balance of the cosmos on more than one occasion. Let's not add another one."

"How does it make you feel when you know things, then you don't? You're a pawn!" Arcadis yelled.

"It matters not what you think of me, Arcadis. But know this, we will meet many more times in the future from your arrogance and stupidity."

"Why tell me if I am going to forget it?"

"Goodbye, Arcadis. I will see you in a few years. And don't worry, when I leave, you will wonder why all of you are here. You'll question it briefly, and then move on."

"And what of you, *Divinius*? Will you be made to forget too?"

"Yes," *Divinius* said as he snapped his fingers and disappeared.

Arcadis looked around. "What am I doing here? The last thing I remember was being in my antique store."

Madame Gildeon looked around too. "The last thing I remember, I was at a meeting. Jackson, is there something you need?"

Jackson looked around and then bowed deeply. "No, Madame Gildeon. I, too, do not know why I am here. I will return to earth."

The sorcerers returned to their daily activities, unaware of what had happened.

*****

Deep inside a labyrinth, far removed from any known realities, two entities emerged.

"Why did you put me through agony and get shot? Why have me almost perish, sire?"

"I needed you to believe your plight was real, so you seemed genuine. Did you do as you were instructed with the sorcerer and the son of *Deus*?"

"Yes, sire!"

"Good. My plan can't fail!"

Learn more about the series:

This story takes place immediately before book one in the renowned *Arcadis Series* (Arcadis Prophecy), with further references to book two (Arcadis War,) book four (Arcadis Emperor of all Emperor of none,) and book six (Arcadis To walk among the gods).

Tea Party

Written by: Adam K. Moore

A loud thump came from overhead as the two tired parents just got settled with their dinner and drinks to watch their favorite TV show before going to bed. This would be the third time one of them had to go upstairs and address the need to go to sleep with their four-year-old daughter, Lily.

"How is she still awake?" asked Lily's mother in exasperation.

"Seriously," sighed Lily's father as he let his head fall back dramatically on the couch. "She had a field day at school, no nap, and then the zoo with your mom and dad." He sat back up and arranged the few items on the coffee table they had brought into the living room with them for dinner. "I'd be out like a light," he thought aloud. "Like I'm gonna be about halfway through eating this…" he paused to examine the food that was in a bowl in front of him. "What exactly are we eating?"

"It's leftover goulash and chili," his wife responded. "It's better with sour cream and cheese. Try it." He followed his wife's instructions and took a bite. "Try it with some crackers. It's even better." He did. She was right, as usual.

"Good idea combining the two," he said sincerely, happy to finally be home and on the couch. "Maybe we can get a sitter tomorrow night and go out," he offered. "Payday."

Another thump came from the ceiling above, and a muffled giggle could be heard as their daughter now seemed to be moving around her room.

"Just… how?" her mother repeated, as if God would answer her directly. "Do you mind going up and checking on her so I can eat? I didn't have anything for lunch today and I'm afraid I might take out my hanger on her," she pleaded to her husband.

He sighed, yet jumped up to show his agreement to go. He may have been a little too obvious that he wasn't happy about it.

"Thanks baaabe," she said, acknowledging that she would stay put while he addressed the needs of their child this time. She had been forced to play bad-cop most of the evening when she got home from work and had to wrangle her daughter to finish her dinner, take her bath, and get dressed for bed.

"Mmm hmm," he replied as he marched up the stairs to his daughter's bedroom.

He quietly approached Lily's bedroom, pausing at the door before entering so he could hear what exactly he would be interrupting. He stood there for a few moments to listen and stared at the artwork plastering the door. One in particular always caught his eye when he would shut the door for the night. It was situated at about waist height, and was drawn mostly with crayon. In neat preschool teacher handwriting, the words "Mommy, Daddy, and Me!" were accompanied by three figures made up of circular lines and marker and whatnot all over the page. He loved this picture, and always looked for it before he had to go in and be a parent.

    He continued to stand there and critique the artwork as he listened to Lily whispering softly on the other side, likely talking to one of her many dolls. Previous trips up the stairs that evening to address Her Highness's many needs had included a snack, then a drink of water, then a potty break, then a drink of water *and* a potty break. This time, she didn't come to the top of the stairs and holler down her request to her parents as she had on previous occasions. He was thankful that, at least for now, she was still in her room. However, he remembered the mission he accepted when he heard a little "clink" that let him know she was playing with her great-great-grandmother's tea set she had recently acquired, and was out of bed.

He thrust open the door and, without hesitation, looked at the table where he expected to see his little girl sitting. But, when his eyes finally adjusted to the small night light in the dimly lit room, she was found sitting upright in her bed with the covers thrown off, looking very innocent. Classic Lily.

He shifted his gaze as he stood in the doorway and said "Hey," somewhat baffled at the sight of seeing her in bed and not at the tiny table in the opposite corner of her room.

"Yeah, daddy?" she replied quietly.

"What are you doing?" he asked rhetorically.

"Just having a tea party, daddy. Do you want to join us?"

Flattered by the invitation but tired of making trips up and down the stairs every few minutes, he shook his head and entered the room to tuck her in… again. "No, sweetheart. It's time for bed like we've been telling you for the past hour."

"I know daddy, but my friend came to play and I didn't want to be rude," she explained, amicably.

He began the timely process of tucking her in for the fourth time as he admonished her. "Well, Lily, your friends know by now when your bedtime is. They should've RSVP'd before 8 PM," he told her, playing along. He was a little proud of himself that he hadn't missed this opportunity. He usually just shook his head and wouldn't take the bait.

"Can you get Polly for me?" Lily asked as he finished tucking the blanket around her just how she liked it. "I dropped her. Please?"

He took a step sideways and snapped up the little plush dolly lying on the floor, dropped in haste no doubt as she had scrambled back to bed.

"Here you go, honey," he said calmly as he tucked the doll into bed with her. "I need you to make me a promise though. Okay?"

"What?" she asked excitedly.

"I need you to stay in bed and go to sleep," he reminded her. Again.

He could see the slightly disappointed look on his daughter's face as she realized they were not about to embark on some secret late-night tea party together.

"But daddy, I don't want to go to bed," she whined. "I want to stay up with my friend."

"You and Polly can stay up and chat and drink tea as long as you're quiet and in bed," he said, caving a little for the benefit of their relationship. She had been really good the past couple days and, despite the challenges at bedtime, was getting high praise from everyone for being such a good listener lately, despite the challenges she gave her mother tonight.

"Oh, Polly doesn't like tea, daddy" she replied, matter-of-factly.

He continued to fuss over the covers attempting to straighten out the folds and creases that weren't addressed during the initial tuck. He shook his head at the ridiculous notion that she got out of bed for a tea party with her doll that doesn't even like tea. "Why the hell would you invite a friend to a party where they aren't even gonna like what's being served," he thought to himself, fighting the urge to blurt out the question to his four-year-old daughter. He was tired.

"Well, silly, then I guess you don't need to be up having a tea party then if Polly doesn't like tea," he replied with a little gentle sarcasm.

"Nooo daddy," she responded as if he didn't know what the hell he was talking about. "The tea wasn't for her. It was for my other friend… the one who lives in the closet."

"Great. Here we go with the closet again," he thought. First, it was scratching noises a few months ago, which turned out to be nothing. Then, it was lightning flashing in the closet, which turned out to be a loose lightbulb with the switch on. Then it was a monster after that, which turned out to be clothes and shadows from things around her room which prompted moving the night light to a different outlet. Now, it's a friend that wants to have tea parties and keep his daughter up past her bedtime. At least she wasn't scared anymore.

"Well at least your friend could be a little quieter so I don't have to keep coming up here to see what is going on," he said as he stood and walked over to the closet to shut the door that was now wide open. "Why did she leave this open in the first place," he wondered out loud, thinking his wife left it open since she was up here last time. The door squeaked lightly and shut with that familiar, delicate "click."

"Mommy didn't leave it open."

"And maybe your friend could bring the tea to you instead of you getting out of bed again," he said, ignoring her retort.

"Assrilll likes to sit at the table, daddy," she said.

"Assrill?" he replied snarkily. Where did she come up with this one he wondered. "Your friend's name is Assrill?"

"Yep, and he likes to drink tea and play games," she said.

"Pft," he snorted, laughing and shaking his head.

"When I'm older," she explained, "he said he would teach me how to play his most favoritist game."

"And what game would that be?" he obliged her, a little afraid to hear what game her imagination had whipped up that is appropriate for a little girl like herself and a male imaginary friend to play.

"Chest," she replied.

"Do you mean chess?"

"I don't know," she said honestly. "It's just his favorite game. Do you know how to play chest, daddy?"

"It's called chess, honey," he said, "and daddy used to play it with his friends."

"I bet I can beat you once I learn," she said with confidence, and waited for his rebuttal.

He warmed his legs with his hands and thanked God it was something as innocent as chess. "Okay, Bobby Fischer," he said, recalling the lengthy discussion he and his wife had in front of Lily last weekend when the power went out and how children missed out on classic board games thanks to video games and cell phones. Though he couldn't honestly remember mentioning chess at any point.

"Who?" she asked.

"Bobby Fi...Nevermind. It's bedtime. Period. Amen," he said and got to his feet after sitting on the bed for the remainder of the discussion. He gently pushed on the closet door again to make certain it was closed in order to prevent any further stimulation of his daughter's imagination this evening.

"He'll just open it againnn," Lily chided.

"Oh, I bet he will," he hissed as he lifted his hands and curled his fingers to resemble claws. He hunched his shoulders and growled lowly as he lunged at his daughter, kissing her numerous times on her face and cheeks, making her giggle and relent to him having the final say on the matter.

"I love you, sweetheart," he cooed.

"I love you too, daddy," she replied in kind.

"Stay in bed," he said waving a finger at her. "Dealio?"

"Deal-e-o, daddy-o," she giggled as she rolled on to her side to try and sleep… again.

He stood up once more and walked toward the door, glancing one last time at the closet to ensure it was closed. He couldn't help feeling a bit creeped out at what his daughter had fabricated. Dear God, what if she wasn't making it all up?

"Everything okay?" his wife asked as he ran down the stairs.

"Yep, all good," he reported as he proudly leapt over the back of the couch to reclaim his spot and eat his food before it cooled any further turning into congealed red and brown sludge.

"What were you two talking about up

there?" she inquired.

"Oh, the usual," he started and took a bite of his dinner. "You know… tea party, Polly, imaginary friends."

"Ahhh," she said knowingly. "She finally told you about the man in the closet, huh?"

He slowed down to chew his food a bit more thoughtfully, then swallowed the bolus after he found the words he was looking for. "She didn't mention it was a man," he said to his wife. "I just assumed it was a boy… or maybe someone a little older, like the neighbor kids."

"No, it's a man… but like a young man," she said as though she had met him. "Did she tell you anything else about him?"

"Well, she told me his name was Assrill," he said with a snort, taking another bite of his food. "I was nervous until I heard her utter that name. Then I was just trying not to laugh and insult her imagin…"

"That's not his name," she said abruptly.

"What do you mean it's not his name?" he

asked incredulously. "That's what she said. I even had to repeat it to make sure I heard her right."

His wife set her food aside and jumped up to run to the kitchen. After a few moments and some shuffling of papers, he heard her footsteps getting louder again indicating she was coming back to the living room. She also leapt over the back of the couch and landed lightly with a piece of paper in her hand.

"His name isn't Assrill, you ass," she said with a laugh. She then handed him what appeared to be a blob of crayon scribbles on a piece of paper, similar to what he observed on a daily basis on his daughter's bedroom door. "His name is Azreal."

He studied the drawing a bit closer than the others she had presented him in the past. He noted the numerous circles and the frequent use of the color black. The figure in this drawing had a surprising amount of detail. Much more than Lily's previous renderings. He looked down and sure enough, in the bottom right hand corner where Lilly usually scrawled her signature was a neatly drawn set of letters drawn in crayon "A-Z-R-A-E-L," he read out loud. "What the hell kind of name is that?" he blurted out. "And what's with all the black crayon?"

"I think it's a character from the Smurfs," she said. "I don't know but check out the muscles on that guy," she teased her husband, jamming her foot under his left glute.

"Yeah...I noticed," he said absent-mindedly, still studying his daughters drawing. It was clearly her finest work to date.

He set the drawing aside and forked the dinner in his bowl before asking, "Do you think this is all a little strange?"

"No, not really," she replied calmly. "I remember having an imaginary friend named Pete when I was about her age. Perfectly normal from what the other parents are telling me."

"So her friends have well-built men wearing black robes hiding in their closets too?"

She grabbed the picture back and examined it. "I guess those lines could be a robe?" she said, scrutinizing the sweeping lines near the torso and legs of the character. "I just thought it was the clothes in the closet. Though I do see the hood."

"Maybe we shouldn't encourage this relationship," he thought aloud, worried about the mental well-being of his little girl. "This seems a little weird even for her," he continued. "Like… we're raising a little… I don't know."

"I don't think it's all that deep, honey," she said sincerely. "I think it's just an expression, or a feeling she drew out on paper." She waited for his reaction, and seeing that he didn't really seem to hear her, she added "It could be you, ya know?"

"Well," he said smiling, "that is flattering. But I'm worried she's not talking to animals, or making up friends her own age," he said looking back at the drawing. "I mean, this thing looks like it came out of Assassin's Creed."

"Dork," she teased.

"Honey, I'm serious," he replied. "I think maybe we should talk to her about this. I mean… are you not worried about this? Am I overreacting?" he wondered aloud.

"I think it's sweet how concerned you are, for one," she said in support. "And two, this is one of the reasons you're just now finding out about him."

"What do you mean? How long have you known about him?" he asked.

"For a couple of weeks," she said, then quickly added, "but it's not like she just blurted out his name and drew this picture. There are others. She's just been reluctant to tell you about him for some reason."

"Really?" he said, his interest piqued. "Did she say why?" he asked, feeling a bit insecure that the two most important women in his life were excluding him from their conversations. He always knew this would happen eventually, but he didn't think it would happen at four years old.

"I think she knew you'd be worried," she said calmly.

"She's only four, and she's worrying about my feelings?"

"She's sensitive," she replied. "And you don't take her seriously when she tells you these things," she pointed out, even though she knew it may be a bit painful for him to hear.

He allowed the silence to fill the room after this comment. He knew she was right, but he wished she had seen the interaction he and Lily just had a few moments ago. They both looked at their meals and took a couple of bites as if they were on their first date again and didn't know what to say to each other.

"Azrael," he said, finally breaking the silence. He wiped his hands on his pants to remove the fine beads of sweat that had started to ooze from his pores as he and his wife tried to solve a parenting problem together. "You think that's from a cartoon?" he asked as he reached for his cell phone, typing the name into the internet search.

"Yeah," responded his wife. "I think it's the name of the bad guy's cat."

"Pretty random reference, don't ya think?" he said skeptically. "Has she even seen the Smurfs?" he asked as he came across the referenced character when he searched for 'Azrael cartoon cat.'

"She's seen all the old cartoons and a lot of what we watched when we were kids," his wife replied passively. "I wouldn't be surprised if she knew who Baby Rose Marie was at this point."

He snorted and nodded his head without looking up from his phone, as if he understood the reference. He then did another web search for the name 'Azrael' and was startled by the new definitions that were populating the small screen he held in his hand.

"What the fu…"

"Babe! Language," his wife reminded him. She was intrigued though and looked over to see what he had discovered. "Oh, Jesus," she said as she saw the descriptions on his phone.

"Not exactly," he replied. "More like 'angel of death.'"

"The angel of death is having tea parties and playing chess with our daughter," she said flatly. "That's the dumbest thing I've ever heard. It's obviously a coincidence, or she's heard of this character from some show or story."

"Still," he argued. "The drawing, and the... the secrecy."

"And we're missing our own show the longer we talk about this," she replied, fatigued from the day and the recent development. "Can we please just watch some TV, eat this reheated garbage, and worry about the angel of death later?" she begged.

"Fine," he replied, putting his phone down on the coffee table and picking up what was left of his dinner. "Okay. We can just talk about it later."

"Thank you," she said as she put her plate down on the table, giving up on dinner and settling for a snuggle with her well-intentioned husband. He continued to eat his food and pushed play on the remote, finally settling in to watch a few minutes of their show before one of them surrendered to sleep.

    Upstairs, Lily lay on her side facing away from her bedroom door right where her daddy had left her. She finally made the decision to follow her parent's instructions and stay in bed this time. She had almost fallen asleep when she heard a familiar sound coming from the closet. There was a low hum, a flicker of light that came out from under the door, then a light click as the door knob turned. The door opened gently and a large, robed figure stepped out of the darkness towards the little girl.

    Lily sat up excited, but concerned that her friend had come back so many times that evening. She had already given him a snack, two cups of water, and let him have the room while she went to the bathroom twice. This was all at his insistence because he said her room was not safe, and he needed reasons to keep her out of there while he dealt with the bad guys. Azrael had made his best efforts to keep these intrusions to a minimum, but there was something about Lily that drew the demons to her like a sacred magnet. He was confident, however, that this would be the last time he needed to interrupt her rest.

"Still," the man said downstairs, not completely willing to let the subject drop yet. His wife sat up sharply and picked up her dinner again, irritated by his obstinance. "What?" he pleaded. "The angel of death, honey!"

"Let it go, please," she begged. "It's just her imagination. It's not unusual for kids her age to dream up imaginary…"

Her plea was interrupted by an unearthly boom that came from within their house. Lily's mother let out a scream and both parents jumped with fright as the noise hit them where they sat. The light fixture hanging from the ceiling above swayed slightly, and a fine dust rained down on the couple as they sat stunned by the noise. They both glanced around the room with their mouths unhinged and jaws dropped. They briefly glanced at each other and bolted from the couch, scrambling to get up the stairs as fast as they could.

"Stop!" he yelled as they got to their daughter's bedroom door before they both rushed in. "Just wait here for a sec," he warned his wife. She agreed and hesitated as instructed while he burst into the room. The room was noticeably darker as Lilly's night-light had been extinguished during whatever had happened up here.

"Lily?" her father managed to choke out half-way between a whisper and a whimper.

There was no response from the room. Lily's bed was empty once again. Only she was not at the table for tea, nor was she in the bathroom getting another drink or going potty.

"Lily?" her mother repeated and worked up the courage to enter the room. No response. She noticed a faint sparkle to the air - as if some of the dust particles had ignited and were glowing a very faint, but visible blue light. If she hadn't been so terrified, it would have seemed pretty to her.

"Hi mommy," came Lily's voice from the closet. Relief flooded into their veins and they rushed over to the closet door that was once again open to assess their only child for injuries. They pushed aside the clothes that were hanging and noticed a slight sulfur smell - like rotten eggs. They assumed Lily must have left some food in a pocket and pushed through the stench toward the bottom of the closet. But after a few moments of digging, they were surprised to come up empty handed.

"Honey," her father said, "we can't see you. Can you come out here for us?"

"I can't, daddy," she replied. "I have to go."

"What?" asked her mother. "Lily please just help us get you out so mommy can look at you and make sure you're okay."

"I'm okay mommy," came her daughter's

voice from inside the closet, yet nowhere in particular. "I'm with Azrael."

The wind was sucked out of her mother's lungs, yet somehow transferred to her father's as he yelled "Lily get out here right now!" He panicked and started throwing clothes out of the closet in heaps. Coats, summer dresses, hats, shoe boxes, and a number of other items flew through the air. They were both emptying the closet of all its contents now, and before long they stared at the stinking, white inner wall of the closet where a large crack had formed. It was about three feet in height and was the obvious source of the stench that had filled their noses, as well as where their daughter's voice was coming from. Similarly to the air around them, there was a faint blue glow to this gash that had formed in the wall.

"I have to go now, daddy," came Lily's voice. "Azrael said it's not safe here."

"You tell Azrael *he* won't be safe if he doesn't bring you back right now!" he yelled, feeling as though he had completely lost his mind. He was yelling at a crack in the wall that had swallowed his daughter and her formerly imaginary friend, the angel of death.

"Baby I need you to stay away from him and come back to your room right now!" pleaded her mother.

There was a brief silence, then a whispered response from her daughter. "They're here mommy. We have to go. I love you. Love you, Daddy-o." Astonished, they both gawked at the empty closet. "Azrael said we'll see you soon," Lily's voice said once more.

"Oh, Jesus! Do something!" screamed Lily's mom. Her dad attempted to dig at the crack in the wall but it didn't seem to make any difference as it seemed to remain the same size despite him clawing at it. At some point during the frantic effort, one of his fingernails separated itself from the nail bed and he began to bleed all over the wall. He hadn't even noticed the pain and continued on until he was sick with fatigue.

In fact, he was starting to feel overwhelmed by the stench emanating from within and had to back away.

Lily's mother decided she would have a go at the jagged opening, but as she scrambled forward to begin, there was a dull rumble as the floor vibrated. She witnessed the crack seal itself from the top down as her hands met the place where it was previously. It was as if she was watching a video of the crack forming rewind, effectively sealing itself without a trace. All that remained were some bloody claw marks from her husband's previous efforts to extricate their daughter from the impossibly narrow opening. Then, silence once again.

"Lily?" asked her mother, pensively, with a whimper.

Silence.

"Lily!" yelled her father.

Silence.

"Lily!" they both yelled in unison.

Silence. Their daughter was gone.

Learn more about the series:

Angels versus demons is a matchup as old as time itself. But when an angel appears next to a nobody like Jacob Curzo (it's a tradition) Crawley on his way to work one morning, life and death suddenly take on a whole new meaning. When guardian angels were suddenly revealed without warning or explanation, nobody seemed worried that the foe – demons – could be right behind them. But Jacob is more important than he realizes, and the information he holds is key to surviving the coming battle for the mortal world.

See the world through Jacob's eyes. The *Compendium Twenty-Three* Series begins with Part I: Through the Valley and continues in Part II: Shadow of Death. Both are available now. Part III: Fear No Evil will see the series come to an end, as well as the world as we know it. (Release date TBD.)

Pygmalion
Written by: Jason Cobalt

Genevieve Simmons has been at the Delta Regional Medical Center ICU for several months. She is in a coma. She is also several months pregnant. A recent scandal at another hospital had prompted a new protocol. No male staff were allowed to be in a room alone with a female coma patient. When the new rule was first announced, it was preemptively coupled with an equal rule, but in reverse, to fend off critical Men's Rights Activists. Security cameras already in the hallways ensured that the rule was followed. It was also standard protocol at the time to administer pregnancy tests for female patients at intake for any and all conditions, no matter who they were. Many found it ridiculous that this included patients well into their eighties, but the hospital felt it was better to be safe than sorry. Genevieve's test was positive. The timing suggested that Miss Simmons was already pregnant when she fell into the coma. That possibly, the coma was a result of the pregnancy itself. As there were no bodily injuries, no foul play was suspected.

Her parents, Ross and Shelby, were grief stricken when the doctors gave them the news that Genevieve would likely never recover. They came under fire from the press when they refused to take her off life support until the baby was born. Protesters admonished them for using their brain-dead daughter as an incubator. The Simmons were undeterred. Genevieve was their only child, and they wanted a part of her to live on. They wanted their grandchild.

When the time came, Genevieve was wheeled into the Operating Room for a cesarean section. Her parents tearfully said their final goodbyes to their daughter. She was to be taken off life support once the baby was out. Despite the controversy, Ross and Shelby's close friends and family were there to show support. Not all of them agreed with their decision, but family was family. At least that's what they said.

Screams came from the OR. The Simmons rushed to the door to see what was the matter, but they were barred entry by the orderlies. Three staff members; a doctor, a nurse, and an assistant bolted out from the double doors. The assistant, a rather large, heavyset fellow, was running away with the speed of a track star. The others kept pace. Their eyes were wide, bugged out. Their mouths were open with the corners turned downward, teeth showing. Their faces showed the look of sheer horror. These people were fleeing for their lives.

The Simmons family was frightened by the scene. Ross was relentless. He demanded entry. He demanded to know what the hell was going on with his daughter and grandchild. One of the orderlies took a peek through the double doors. He turned around and threw up. The other orderlies tended to their friend, allowing Ross and Shelby the chance to go inside.

Inside the OR, the surgeon was passed out. The two other staff members were cowering in the corners in yellow puddles of their own making, with some brown swirled in. In the center of the room was their daughter, Genevieve, still cut open and completely flatlined. And lying atop her legs, with umbilical cord still attached was the child. But this was no ordinary child.

The baby girl had grey skin and a head of jet-black hair. Her ears jutted with a slight outward lean and came to a point. Her mouth had fangs for the top and bottom canines, at least one of which had already punctured her lip. She had short red claws on her hands and feet. When she opened her eyes, they both had black sclera, red irises, and black pupils.

Ross and Shelby were horrified. They

didn't believe that this was their grandchild. They didn't believe that this was a human child at all. They thought what the others who had seen her must've thought. That this wasn't a baby. This was a demon, straight from the bowels of Hell itself.

Cheyenne Pargett was working at the facility that night. She was a fairly new nurse at the time. A creole from New Orleans who was working a stint at DRMC on contract. She had heard the commotion and rushed in as others were running away. There was pandemonium on the floor. Most of the Simmons' friends and family had already fled.

Cheyenne walked in through the double doors and saw the baby. Ross and Shelby were in the room. They were demanding answers. Cheyenne ignored them. She crossed herself, and sprang into action. She cut the cord and smacked the baby's backside. The baby didn't cry, only whimpered a little. But she was breathing on her own. Cheyenne cleaned the baby off, put her on the cart, and wheeled her to the NICU. Ross and Shelby followed for a few steps, cursing Cheyenne and their grandchild. Those left in the waiting room looked on in horror at the sight of the child. Cheyenne had heard Ross say that he was going to kill the demon the first chance he got.

No one else was brave enough to even touch the baby. Fearing the worst for the child, Cheyenne uttered some words under her breath and the crowd fell silent. They were frozen in place. She said some more seemingly unintelligible words and left with the child. Cheyenne kept chanting the whole way, through the elevator, the parking garage, and into her car. She never stopped chanting, even when she pumped gas a few miles from the hospital.

Cheyenne kept chanting, for five more hours. She had driven all the way from Greenville, Mississippi to her parents' house in New Orleans. She picked up the baby out of the backseat and sprinted to the door. She frantically rang the doorbell and banged on the door with her right hand, the left cradling the newborn girl. The baby was a little fussy, but not crying at the moment. It was still the dead of night.

An older man answered the door. He was tall and thin. His hair was black, but heavily salted and bald on top. It was her father, Malachi. He was surprised to see his daughter, and shocked to see what she was carrying. Not frightened, just shocked. He took a second to snap out of it, and let them inside, his left hand pressing slightly on his daughter's right shoulder blade, nudging her into the house.

Malachi, exasperated, asked, "Baby Girl, what have you done?"

"I know, Daddy, but look at her. They were afraid of her. They were going to kill her. I couldn't let that happen."

"How did you get out with her and not be followed?"

"I did some incantations."

Malachi, hoping Cheyenne had covered

all her bases, asked, "Which incantations?"

"I made anyone who ever saw her or me tonight forget what they saw. And I cast stealth spells every breath of the way here."

"And the security cameras?"

She responded "Should be nothing but static. I put a hex on the full day's tapes."

"Good girl. Who knows you were working tonight? It's got to be in their computers."

"That's the one thing I didn't have a spell for, Daddy. What can we do?"

"That wasn't the only thing you forgot, Baby Girl. But don't worry, I got you. Papa's gonna take care of it. Delores!"

Delores Pargett came down the stairs wearing a night gown. She had heard the commotion but didn't yet know what it's about. She started speaking, to both her husband and daughter. She didn't yet see the child.

Delores started in on Malachi and Cheyenne, "What in the hell are you two doing makin' all this racket at three in the godda-"

She almost tripped mid-sentence when she saw the baby, "Oh my God!"

Delores righted herself, "Good God, Baby Girl, what is that? Is that a baby?"

"Yes, mom, it's a baby. A human baby."

Malachi shook his head, "I don't know about all that."

Cheyenne snapped back, "Well I do. I cut the cord, the umbilical cord, that connected her to her very human mother. I don't know of any science *OR* magic that could make that otherwise."

Malachi disagreed, "Oh there's magic that'll do it alright. Best believe that, Baby Girl. Not a lot of folks around these parts with that kind of magic though. Hell, I don't even think I could do it myself."

Delores noticed something, "It's eerily quiet."

Cheyenne chided her mother, "She, mother. Not an it. She's a she."

Delores turned to her husband, "Well,

what the hell are we gonna do with her, Malachi?"

Malachi cupped his chin with his right thumb and index finger, "Hmmm. Let's see. Well, Baby Girl here took away a lot of our options. Can't complain 'bout it none. I probably wouldn't have done much different. We can't just give her back. We could turn her over to the police. Baby Girl, how do you feel about prison?"

Cheyenne did not appreciate the joke, "Not in the mood, Dad."

Malachi turned to Delores, somewhat giddy, "Oooh, it's Dad now. It's Dad when she mad, but when you were banging on the door earlier, it was Daddy."

Delores punched Malachi on the arm, "Stop it, Malachi. Get serious."

Malachi toned it down, "Alright, alright. Serious now. Long story short, we have to keep her. Her family now don't even remember that she exists, and if they did would probably have killed her if what Baby Girl says is true. We can't turn her over to the authorities. That's just the same thing at this point. And this child is obviously magical in nature. I don't know how, but I can feel it coming off her. Can't y'all?"

Delores and Cheyenne nodded in agreement.

Malachi continued, "We are duty bound to take this child in. We'll have to raise her as our own. The magical community will embrace her, but the outside world will not. We'll need to take care to keep those two worlds separate where she's involved. And maybe, just maybe God willing, some good will come of this."

Cheyenne's own son and daughter, Loras and Aria, were still young and living in the house with Delores and Malachi. Malachi and Delores' son, Walt, was a freshman in college in California. The house was big. It had plenty of room. That wasn't the problem. Delores wasn't crazy about the idea of taking on a newborn, but she couldn't refute Malachi's logic. He was right. The baby girl was innocent, and she was in danger.

Delores reached out her hands, "Baby Girl, I'll take her. You go on and get you some sleep. Malachi, you're going on a diaper run."

Malachi protested, "But it's four in the morning?"

Delores shot him a glare, "Don't you play dumb with me, Malachi. Sam's Club is open twenty-four hours a day and you know it. But don't worry, I'll make you a list."

Malachi huffed before acquiescing. Delores took the infant into the kitchen and wrapped her in a towel for the time being. She wrote the list for Malachi and then rummaged through the foyer closet for some of Loras and Aria's old baby clothes. Malachi left for the store. Cheyenne went to bed. Delores dressed the infant, went to the parlor, sat down on the large padded chair, and rested, cradling the baby girl.

Dawn broke as Malachi returned home. The house was in full view. The main body of the mansion was royal purple. The roof and shutters were dark green. The columns supporting the veranda roof were golden yellow. The landscaping had always featured an array of purple, green, and gold flowers. The trees on the property yielded golden yellow blooms. The house was built by Rexford Pargett right after the Civil War, and added on over the years. It was said that the house took on the Mardi Gras colors, but one of many family secrets was that it was the other way around. A sign hung from the edge of the veranda roof to the front of the main entrance. A black sign with gold lettering fastened at both ends, providing the name of the house. The sign read Galarie d'Ombre.

Malachi decided to call in from work. He was an insurance executive and highly experienced practitioner of magic. He frequently used magic for financial reasons, but never with malevolent intent against other people. Whenever it was possible to gain for himself at no expense to others, he did so. This was allowed in the world's magical community, so long as it didn't adversely affect the other practitioners or make waves in the outside world. Most often, he charmed his policies so that clients could continue to pay their premiums, but never need to make a claim. This kept his firm dominant in the local market and made Malachi a wealthy man, like so many of the Pargetts that came before him. On occasion, Malachi used magic for gambling, though that was frowned on by the magical community. He was at SuperBowl XLIV when the New Orleans Saints upset the Indianapolis Colts in a surprising second half comeback. Though Malachi still swears he had nothing to do with the outcome.

When he got into the house, he saw Delores and the baby asleep on the chair. It had been a long night for everybody. He attempted a maneuver. It had been many years since he attempted this particular trick. Though not magical, it was still very delicate. When Cheyenne and Walt were babies, Malachi had mastered the art of extracting them from Delores' arms while she was asleep, waking neither baby or Delores. He was even quite adept at it when Loras and Aria were that little. But the man was years out of practice, and it showed. A failure on both counts.

The child's wailing woke up the whole house. She was loud. Louder than any baby any of them had ever heard. Her scream had an eerie pitch to it, like it was barely human. The chandeliers in the foyer and parlor were vibrating. Delores got up from her chair, shot Malachi an angry look, and took the baby back from him. She bounced the baby up and down, speaking to her softly. Malachi put up both hands. He made a gesture in each, connecting his thumb with the middle and ring fingers.

"Don't you do it, Malachi! I got this."

Malachi could barely hear his wife, but he knew enough to put his hands down. Delores knew he was about to cast a sleeping spell, something she absolutely forbade with the children and grandchildren. In time, she got the baby quiet.

Cheyenne ran down the stairs. Her kids came down as well. Everyone was still in their pajamas, except for Malachi.

Aria asked, "Who is that, Mommy?"

Cheyenne struggled for an answer, "That's... um..."

Malachi interrupted, "That's your new sister, Aria."

Cheyenne shot him a look.

Malachi snapped back, "Don't give me that look. This one's on you, Baby Girl."

Loras asked, "What's her name?"

Malachi looked to Loras, "That's a good question." He looked to Cheyenne with an inquisitive look, saying nothing.

Cheyenne looked to Delores, "Um. Mom. Any ideas?"

Delores shook her head, "Nope. Baby Girl, your Daddy's right. This one's on you."

Cheyenne lowered her head, "Damnit."

Delores spoke sternly, trying not to shout,

"Watch your mouth, Little Mama, your kids are right there."

"Alright, Mama. Hey, what's that one show you like? The one with the four white ladies from Georgia? I think they run some kind of decorating company?"

Delores pondered, "I know the one you're talking about. Can't think of the name though. Why?"

"I liked it too. I really liked the sister. The sassy one. What was her name?"

Delores replied, "I don't remember the character's name, but the actress' name was Delta."

The baby seemed to smile at the suggestion.

Cheyenne wasn't sure. "I don't know, Mama. That's the name of the hospital she was born in."

Malachi had noticed the smile, "She seems to like it. Kind of fitting. She was born in the Delta. The region, not the hospital."

"So were all of us, Dad. What do I tell her when she asks how she got her name?"

Malachi crossed his arms and smiled as he answered, "Baby Girl, you just tell her that you named her after that nice lady who was married to Major Dad."

Everyone shot Malachi a look. The grown-ups all busted out laughing. The kids had no idea what they were talking about.

Cheyenne made it official, "Delta it is." She squatted down to get at Delta's eye level. "What do you think of that?"

Delores answered, "I don't know what she thinks about the name, but I know she needs to be changed."

As the years went by, Delta grew faster than most kids. By the time she was five, she was eye level with Loras, who was thirteen at the time. By age fifteen, she was as tall as Malachi, who stood six foot even. She was lanky as a teenager, but as a young woman, Delta not only kept her demonic appearance, but also had the build of a natural female bodybuilder.

Delta grew into a powerful user of magic; the most naturally gifted Malachi had ever seen by far. She was casting successful spells not long after first learning to speak. She was world famous in the magic community, all the while the outside world was completely unaware of her existence. She had no birth certificate or social security number due to the unusual circumstance of her birth and subsequent abduction. Adults in the community absolutely idolized her. They marveled at her accomplishments, even from a young age.

Delta was homeschooled, mostly by Malachi and Cheyenne. Malachi taught her magic. Cheyenne taught her everything else, as magic users required at least a solid working knowledge of language, arts, and STEM. By the time she was a preteen, Delta had surpassed even Malachi's abilities. From then on, Malachi brought in magic tutors from all over the world. They were all well compensated, but most would have done it for free simply for the honor of having taught Delta something.

Delta underwent lots of memory training. The vast majority of magical training had to be taught from mouth to ear. The world's magical community had strict rules about what was allowed to be written down. Families were only permitted to have one written volume, and only for their own spells. Whenever the book was full, that was it. The Pargetts developed their own shorthand to conserve space in their ancestral text. Delta was rapidly filling pages with her own spells. Speaking or writing about magic into any electronic device was strictly forbidden, ever since the early days of the telegraph.

Despite all the adulation from the magic community, Delta was still very lonely. She never got to just play with other kids, even the ones from magic families, for obvious reasons. Her appearance and her abilities made it difficult for those around her, except for the Pargetts, to see her as the child that she really was. Expectations were always high, and there was never time for silly games, even with kids her own age.

Hurricane Katrina was the first real test of her power. She and Malachi were in Wyoming at the time training with a Native American medicine man. Malachi loved these indigenous people so much, he named his only daughter after them, Cheyenne. The training was three days long. They were miles away from civilization and had no communication with the outside world. But Delta didn't need a phone, when she felt Delores reach out to her. Delta, picking up on Delores' unique aura, was able to astral project thousands of miles away back to the Galarie d'Ombre. The house already had several protection spells cast onto it over the years. Delta was able to cast hers much further. Her neighborhood was saved. The surrounding areas were not as lucky. Delta and Malachi would forever feel guilty afterward for being away during that time. Had Delta been physically present, and not had to devote a part of her concentration to her projection, she could've protected the whole city and no one would be the wiser. New Orleans would've believed it was a miracle, and in a way they'd have been right.

Delta had to live a secluded life due to her appearance. She understood the reasons and took her predicament in stride. But she was still lonely. Deep down, she was still just a little girl.

Social media became a thing when Delta was a teen. Through it, she cultivated an online life for herself to replicate the one she couldn't have in the real world. She'd take photos of her trips with Malachi and post them on her profiles, sans any personally identifiable information. By necessity, the Pargetts had become expert at participating in this digital world without leaving a traceable footprint; the NSA could've learned a lot from them.

Through social media, Delta's personality was able to shine through. Even when she was in her twenties, her demeanor was still that of a teenager due to her secluded upbringing. She was a world class expert in magic, and had a good working knowledge about many topics. But she was deeply naive about subjects like sex and relationships.

Delta was an avid reader and a movie buff. Her online peers followed her advice on what to read and watch. She loved online gaming, especially the MMORPGs, often taking the name Dark Elf Queen. In adventure games, she'd craft characters that looked like her and put them in sexy outfits and adorn them with ornate jewelry. She'd blush when other players referred to her as hot. She had never felt desirable before. The compliments were a boost to her self-esteem, but she was still very careful to not reveal too much about herself.

Later, Delta learned how to disguise her physical appearance with a glamour spell. She chose the form of a young creole woman who looked similar to her adoptive family. She'd present this to Malachi as proof that she was ready to face the outside world. He reminded her that cameras are everywhere and that even he didn't yet know a spell that could keep her out of all of them. A single device was easy to fool as long as one knew it was there. The technology spells they'd developed worked because they cast them on their own computers and phones. Even then, some magic users were slipping up, getting caught on camera. A skeptical public normally passed them off as fake. Governments outside the US were rounding up these people and their families. It was still too great a risk to take.

One day, a depressed Delta was playing an online adventure game. On one of her quests, she came across a player she'd never seen before, but who had amassed one of the highest levels in the game. She knew all the heavy hitters from all over the world. This player was new and a complete stranger. His avatar had the body of an Olympic swimmer, milky white skin, with blue eyes and blue hair. The screen name shown above him simply read "Charlie".

A private message text box appeared next to him. It said, "Hello, Delta. I've been looking for you."

Learn more about the series:

This entry is chapter three of what is meant to be a three-part series exploring a more grounded take on the superhero genre. The main cast of characters are a diverse group of individuals presented as a means to question conventional wisdom and turn understood ideas about race, religion, and sexuality on their heads. Their backgrounds and motivations vary wildly. This fictional world operates under more realistic circumstances than other such stories in the genre. The super powered people within it have the same kinds of goals, motivations, and beliefs as would any 'normal' person, if such a thing truly exists. A major aim of the project is to conceptualize the real-world ramifications of such beings; including practical application, social/political implications, and more realistic physical consequences.

Blood Dragon: The Search Begins
Written by: Katheryn Schwarz

The cave reeked of must. Light seemed to emanate from the air itself, just enough to see by. In the distance, I could hear the plink of water drops hitting a pool. Panic filled me. *It's this dream again.* Sandra turned to me, her hand beckoning for me to follow, her grin innocent and playful.

"Come on, you amazon!" Her voice echoed off the walls, soft and as playful as her smile.

I shook my head, backing away.

"What, you don't want to find out what's at the end of this tunnel?" She asked. "It's a fun surprise." Her luminescent eyes were alight with mischief now.

No, no, no, no, I have to get out.

Without a word, I turned to run. Sandra was in front of me still, her hand on her hip, a furious look on her face.

"My family will get what we're owed, Kayla. It's just a matter of time. You being the Blood Dragon is just a bonus." Her voice was dark, her brown eyes glowing in the dim light of the cave.

I glanced behind me, and Sandra was there again, "Come with me, Kayla. You don't have to be afraid."

"On the contrary," the angry Sandra said, "You should be terrified." From under her jacket, she produced an intricate ritual dagger, the black blade curved slightly as if it were made from a Dragon's claw.

With a shriek, I sat up in bed, panting for breath. My hand clutched at my shirt, trying to steady my racing heart.

Zeke rolled over, his arm lazily wrapping around my hips and pulling me close. He peered at me through one half-opened, amber eye. "Was it the dream again?" His voice was thick with sleep.

Taking another shaky breath, I nodded. "It was. Each time it's just a little different. Sometimes she's there, sometimes she's not. Sometimes she's everywhere."

"Which was it tonight?"

"Everywhere," I said solemnly.

Zeke sat up, the covers falling away from him and pooling into his lap, with an almost liquid-like fluidity.

"I know it is no consolation, but these dreams will eventually pass." He spoke through a yawn, wrapping his arms around me and pulling me back down into the bed.

I nodded again and snuggled into his embrace. "I know. I just wish it'd happen sooner."

Zeke merely hummed in response, petting my hair in soothing strokes until sleep engulfed me once again.

When I woke in the morning, Zeke was sitting on the edge of the bed, pulling on his shoes.

"Ah, Kayla. I was wondering when you would wake up." He turned and smiled at me at the sound of me stirring. "Did you sleep well?"

"The second half of my sleep was pretty nice."

"Good."

"Where are you going?" I asked, checking the time on my phone. It was 7:30 in the morning.

"I have a meeting with Trace. Would you like to come?"

I wasn't sure what to make of the words. A few months ago, they wouldn't have made sense, since Trace used to be one of Xander's right-hand men.

Then again, this last year made little to no sense, comparatively.

I used to be a logger. A lumberjack, if you will. I was in a happy relationship with a cute lawyer woman named Sandra, until she turned out to be the lawyer for the Dragon Mafia, and was using me to get information and had me abducted by Trace and his now-dead buddy Don, for her father -- Xander, the leader of the Dragon Mafia. Now, how did I not piece two and two together? The Dragon Mafia is very good at keeping their faces out of the media. The day before I'd been abducted, I'd had this crazy nightmare where I was in a cave with Sandra, and she was leading me to the back of the cavern, where her father stabbed me with an ornate blade, and it was now a recurring nightmare, that was slightly different each time I had it. Sometimes she was there, sometimes Xander was, sometimes no one was there, sometimes they both were. Either way, it was a terrifying experience. Anyway, when I'd been abducted, I'd suffered Chloroform poisoning and a severe concussion, along with some pretty hefty bleeding. I'd escaped through sheer willpower, and hid in the back of Zeke's truck, not knowing it was his, nor that he would change my life forever. He found me, and saved me. And also turned me into a Dragon. But not just any ol' Dragon, no. He turned me into the Blood Dragon -- someone fated to save the world from something called the Great Undoing.

See, Dragons are real, and I didn't know this beforehand. They used to have their majestic fantasy-filled forms, until the Celestial Gods made the Great Sacrifice to their god -- The Old Sky, Creator of All -- to save Dragons from being killed off by Humans. The Old Sky warned that one day a Dragon would come along who would be daft enough to try to undo the Great Sacrifice, which would undo all of creation, but that a Dragon would be created -- not born, *created* -- through trauma and sacrifice, and would either stop the Great Undoing, or become part of it. And thus my fate was sealed. Being abducted, trauma. My family being killed off by Xander and his goons? Still trauma. Probably some form of sacrifice. Unless we get real deep and consider me giving up all of my ties to Humanity in order to learn everything there is to know about Dragon Magic to protect the world from Xander's selfishness. I don't really know. I try not to think too much about it, because it makes me depressed.

So while I sat at the edge of the bed, thinking over all of these things and trying to think about what to wear today, Zeke snapped me out of my funk.

"Kayla. Would you like to come with me to the meeting with Trace?"

"Oh. Uh, yes." I stood up, walking to my wardrobe and pulling out the first clothes my hands landed on.

"Are you not going to even *try* to match?" Zeke asked incredulously.

Despite how close we'd grown, and that we were now an unspoken couple, Zeke still couldn't get over that I dressed like, well, a lumberjack. Plaid, jeans, boots.

"Why? It's not like we're meeting with the

Celestial Gods." *And even then, I probably wouldn't care to dress any differently,* I finished my statement internally.

Zeke closed his eyes, pinching the bridge of his nose. "Gods, you are something else."

"You still love me."

"Always."

I threw on my clothes with reckless abandon, flipping my hair out from under my shirt and undoing the braid, only to redo it so it didn't look like I had slept in it. When I pulled on my boots, my stomach growled.

"Please tell me we're meeting him at the diner."

"Indeed we are."

"Finally, cheap coffee and cheaper waffles." I sighed. The diner still gave me the creeps, since Janine had drugged and abducted me there. I was beginning to notice a recurring theme in my life this last year.

"You can have coffee and waffles here."

"It's not the same!"

"If you insist," Zeke relented with a sigh. He was irritable this morning, likely from the lack of sleep after I'd had my nightmare.

I stood up, wrapping my arms around Zeke, deciding to ask him. "Did you not sleep well after my nightmare?"

"I did not. You kept tossing and turning in bed." He embraced me for a moment to show me he wasn't agitated with me.

We walked arm-in-arm down the halls to the entryway. The door beeped as it shut behind us. We climbed into Zeke's truck, and we were off to the diner.

The drive took a while, as Zeke lived away from town. We made idle conversation to pass the time.

"Have you heard anything from Desmond and Molly since last week?" I asked.

"No, I have not. Have you?" He replied, sparing me a glance.

I shook my head. "Not since Molly kicked us out. It's really weird. I feel like she's hiding something, but I can't imagine what."

"I cannot imagine, either." Zeke was rubbing his chin with his left hand, steering with his right.

Our conversation fell into contemplative silence after that, Zeke likely mulling over all the ideas of where Desmond and Molly may had run off to, just as I was. I didn't know as much about the dynamic duo of Ascended Dragons as Zeke did, considering they weren't my grandparents, but rather his, although I had a few ideas. And worries.

We pulled into the parking lot for the diner. I saw Trace leaning against his sleek blue car, smoking a cigarette. He stamped it out as soon as he saw us pulling up to our spot.

"I didn't know you smoked," I said as I stepped out of the truck.

Trace shrugged. "Gotta pass the time somehow," He said.

"Don't those things give you cancer?" I asked.

Trace looked at me quizzically. He blinked a few times before suddenly saying, "Oh, right. You used to be *Human.* I forgot." With a short laugh, he continued, "Dragons don't get cancer."

"All the stuff in cigarettes though, that's gotta be bad for you." I crossed my arms.

Trace shrugged. "Human scientists don't know anything about Dragons, and I'd like to keep it that way."

"What about Dragon scientists?" I asked.

He shrugged again. "We don't test on our kind like Humans do. We use our abilities t'fix each other up, so the Human marvels of 'modern medicine' are, frankly, unique t'humanity alone."

I looked to Zeke for affirmation, and he just nodded. "Trace is correct. You were a very unique case, since you *were* Human when I found you."

"How did you know what to do to save my life?"

It was Trace's turn to look between me

and Zeke, open interest on his face.

"I read more than just the lore of my people. Human medicine is highly fascinating."

I made a noncommittal noise, nodding. "We should get inside. It looks like rain is going to come soon."

"Oh, is the Blood Dragon scared of gettin' a little rain on her?" Trace asked.

Zeke offered his arm, and I took it, leaning into him gratefully.

"No, but I don't want my hair getting frizzy."

Trace laughed at my remark, but moved with us as we started walking toward the door. I held the door open for him, and we spent a moment bickering about who was supposed to enter first.

"Ladies first."

"I'm holding the door, I didn't have to get it for you."

"It's ladies, then gentlemen. That's how I was raised."

"And I was raised to hold the door for the person behind you, regardless of their gender."

Zeke released my arm and held the door open for a woman who was trying to leave the diner, then stared pointedly at us. "How about you both go in, and I hold the door?" He asked dryly.

Trace and I looked at each other, then shrugged and walked into the diner. I let the door shut behind me, and Zeke sighed in exasperation.

"Dealing with you two is like dealing with children."

"Hey!" Trace and I said in unison.

Zeke rolled his eyes. "Point and case."

As we filed inside the diner, a passing waitress waved. "Hello! Seat yourselves, and I'll be right with you."

We all acknowledged her in our respective ways -- Zeke and I nodding, and Trace smiling and waving back -- then headed to a table in an unoccupied corner of the restaurant. We pulled out menus and began to peruse them.

"Why are you looking at the menu when you already know what you want?" Zeke asked after a few minutes.

"It's the principle of the thing," I objected.

Trace shook his head. "My dear, you dun have t'look at the menu if you already know what you want."

"It's the principle of the thing," I reiterated, setting the menu down. "Plus, I like to get ideas for next time."

"Don't you order the same thing every time?" He asked.

"She does," Zeke replied, sounding more tired than his years.

The waitress came by. "What can I get you guys to drink this morning?" She asked brightly.

She was a pretty little thing, standing at about five-foot-five, and thin. Her raven hair was pulled back into a messy bun, and her eyeliner was done in sharp wings that looked like they could cut you if you got too close. She had dimples when she smiled, and bright green eyes.

"Coffee for me, please," I said.

"I will have a coffee as well, please," Zeke seconded.

"Make that three coffees, please, ma'am." Trace turned up his southern charm, grinning at the waitress. She blushed at him, then rushed off.

Zeke stood up after the waitress left, pulling his buzzing phone out of his pocket. "I will return shortly. I must take this call."

"Already moving on, Trace?" I asked playfully once Zeke had left hearing range.

"Oh, you know you're the only girl for me. I can't help when a pretty girl blushes at my handsome smile."

"You know the whole 'flirt with other girls to make them jealous' thing doesn't work on me, right?" I asked, leaning my cheek into my hand. "I'm not gonna go anywhere, Zeke's stuck with me."

"So you say, but you waited until after he left to say somethin'." His dark brown gaze met mine, and I felt my stomach knot.

"That's because Zeke *does* get jealous," I said flippantly.

"Maybe for good reason." He tilted his head to the side, and the way the light bounced off his dark cheekbones made them stand out more. He had no business being charming and handsome, especially after abducting me the first time we met and trying to keep me abducted the second time we met. But here we were, having a civil conversation. Exchanging playful banter, even. Banter, yes. Not flirting. Definitely not flirting.

"For no *good* reason." I shrugged. "Zeke is about all I have left, since Desmond and Molly disappeared."

Trace's eyes turned sympathetic. "Yes, I remember. Your parents."

"Did you…?" Kill them? Have something

to do with it? Abduct them too? I didn't have the heart to actually ask the questions.

"No. Xander had someone else handle it. But it was a big deal." Maybe it was his southern drawl, or maybe it was the reassuring tone he took, but something about the way he said it made me feel better.

He must have caught my sullen gaze.

"I'll spare you the details. Instead, give me the details about the Ascended ones."

"You mean you don't know?" I asked.

"No. I haven't heard anything through the grapevine, and if they had been caught somehow, I would definitely have heard. And I would definitely have said something."

"Well, that checks that off our list of possibilities…" I murmured just as Zeke returned. "Desmond and Molly disappeared a couple of weeks ago. We're thinking they skipped town, but we aren't sure."

"No, if Xander captured them, he would have made a show of it. He loves gloating."

Trace's face turned serious.

Zeke looked between me and Trace, then took his seat. The waitress came and set our coffee cups down in front of us.

"There you go." She beamed a second too long at Trace. "Are you guys ready to order?"

"Oh, ah, yes. I'll take the waffles with blueberries, please," I said.

"I will have the crepes special, please." Zeke didn't look up from his phone, his thumbs flying across the screen at lightning speed.

"I'll take the chicken fried steak, please, ma'am." Trace folded his hands in front of him on the table, meeting her gaze.

She blushed again, and said, "I'll have that order for you all right away," then turned and walked away, casting a glance back to Trace.

"I think she has a crush on you, Trace. You should go for it." I jerked my head toward the waitress, who was still in our line of sight.

"Hmm. I'll consider it. Though it's rude t'assume she's immediately interested just 'cause she blushes. She could just be easily flustered."

"No, she's into you," Zeke said, still not looking up from his phone. "Her thoughts are preoccupied with how cute she thinks you are."

"Why are you reading her mind?" I asked.

"Practice is the only way I am going to Ascend."

"Well, it's rude to do it without consent."

"Even if I did have her consent, she is not hiding her thoughts very well. She is projecting them pretty loudly." Zeke shrugged.

"Well if that ain't a moral dilemma, if I ever saw one," Trace said.

Zeke paused his texting, glancing up to meet Trace's gaze. "I do not wish to hear about moral quagmires from you."

"Woah, what's the deal? Didn't you set up this meeting with Trace?" I asked.

"That does not mean I wish to hear the up

and up on morality from him." Zeke resumed texting.

"I'm sorry, Trace. Zeke didn't get much sleep last night--"

"No thanks to you."

"--And he's not exactly at his happiest right now." I turned to Zeke. "Why don't you have some coffee? It'll help you feel better."

Zeke glanced at me as if he were about to say something, but decided against it and raised his coffee mug to his lips while still texting with his other hand.

"So," Zeke began, after a long sip of his coffee, "Desmond and Molly are missing." He finally set his phone down. "And none of your contacts know anything about it?"

"I could spread the word and ask 'bout it, but that might provoke Xander into action, knowing you are weaker without the two most powerful livin' Dragons to help protect you." Trace sighed, "I trust them to give me information, but I dun trust them *with* information, if you understand my meaning."

"That makes sense," I said. Turning to Zeke, I saw that he had a perturbed look on his face and his focus was on the window. I followed his gaze to find that a nondescript black car was parked in the middle of the road, idling outside of the diner parking lot.

Two gentlemen, from what I could see, were gesturing wildly to each other.

"Trace, do you trust your sources to not rat you out?" I asked.

"I mean, half the time they dun know it's me askin' the questions," he responded.

"What about the other half?" I asked again.

"What are you gettin' at?" He demanded.

I gestured to the window behind him. He blanched when he turned, then suddenly got up, downing the rest of his coffee, and rushed to the bathroom.

"Why's he going in there?" I whispered to Zeke.

"He is hiding," Zeke responded coolly.

"How enlightening. A coward," I mumbled.

The car moved, inching forward and into the parking lot. It parked haphazardly in one of the handicapped spots, and the two men got out. They walked purposefully to the entrance, not seeming to care that they were parked like massive dicks.

The door chimed as it swung open and they entered the building. They scanned the dining area and, when their gaze landed on us, they turned slowly and approached our table.

"Zeke Fleetwing. Kayla Cochikev." The taller of the two men said, his face a careful mask of neutrality.

The shorter of the two men spoke next. "We're going to need you two to come with us. The boss wishes to see you."

"And which boss would that be?" I narrowed my eyes, taking in their appearances. They were dressed formally, way too nice to be in a shady diner.

The shorter man's eyes flitted to me. Bright green, with flecks of gold in them. "Why, The Black Dragon, of course." He smirked, though he was in no position to.

The Black Dragon was another name for Xander Blackblood, so named because of his ruthless nature rather than his name.

I crossed my arms under my chest. "And what makes you think we'll be coming with you, willing or not?"

Short Man's smirk widened and he pulled a gun from under his coat, cocking it with more familiarity than I was used to seeing from a Dragon operating a firearm. He gestured with his head to the hostess that was standing behind her podium, and blissfully unaware of the danger she was now in.

"I will start killing everyone in this diner." He looked at the door, and the taller man went over and locked it.

"Sir, I'm going to have to ask you to unlock that door. The doors must remain unlocked during business hours." I could faintly hear the hostess saying. She sounded bored, as if she had to go through this more often with small children than with adults.

Taller Man pulled a gun from his coat pocket, and pointed it at her. She went pale, too terrified to even scream.

"So what is it going to be, Blood Dragon?"

I looked at Zeke, and he nodded. In a flash, too fast to see, he was in front of the man who had his gun pointed at the hostess. At the same time, I stepped forward and disarmed the shorter man. Once the gun was safely tucked away in the back of my jeans, I swept low and kicked his feet out from underneath him, barely missing being punched in the face.

The look on his face as he fell to the floor was priceless. The moment I had to dodge a sudden bolt of flames was not as priceless. I swept the fire up under my control and turned it around to him. He tried to get up, and I stomped the ground, forcing the concrete up and over him, trapping him underneath.

Patrons screamed, waitresses ran into the back, the hostess looked on in horror as if she couldn't believe what was going on. A few of the braver teenagers (or foolish, if you would rather hear it put more simply) stepped forward with their phones out, recording the fighting.

Shorter Man, the one I was fighting with, was struggling to get out of the grasp of the earth I'd pulled around him. I knelt down to get to his level.

"Oh, a wee little fire Dragon?" I asked, mockingly. "And you thought you could take on me?"

"Last we were told, you had only mastered fire." He grunted, fidgeting inside the cement, "Had we known, we would have sent the stronger ones."

I felt a smirk tugging at the corner of my lip. "You were told wrong."

"I can... Tell." He grunted again, straining hard against the earth, with no avail.

Standing up again, I willed the earth to spit him out and reassemble itself. There were tears in the carpet, but Zeke and I could handle the repairs.

"That was a foolish move," the shorter man said, drawing back his fists and lighting them with flames.

I rolled my eyes and swiped the flames out, pulling my own fist back and decking him right in the temple. He hit the floor, stone cold.

"I don't think it was." I muttered.

Looking around, I saw Zeke had long since floored the taller man. I surveyed the damage we'd done to the store, and estimated the cost would be in the thousands. I went over to Zeke and nudged him.

He stepped toward the hostess, who flinched back.

"Wh-What are you?" She asked.

"That doesn't matter," I said. "What matters is that you're safe now."

"This is my card," Zeke said, handing her

a business card with his phone number and email address on it. "When your boss gets the estimated cost of repairs, send the bill to me. I will cover the damages."

"O-Okay." She nodded slowly, her voice sounding distant and far away. I watched as she tucked the business card into her apron pocket, then slowly turned and walked to the back, away from us.

Zeke walked to the table, dropped a one-hundred-dollar bill onto it, then went to the bathroom to recover Trace.

I pulled out my phone and called the police to let them know that "the store had faced an attempted robbery by two members of the Dragon Mafia." They arrived at lightning speed, with SWAT in tow. I unlocked the door for them, and let them in.

"It looks and smells like a natural disaster hit," the officer commented. She was a short, blue-eyed woman that carried herself as if she were my height. Even as a human, she was not someone I wanted to get on the bad side of.

"I laughed it off. "The things that happen during brawls, am I right?"

She looked at me as if she didn't believe a word of what I just said. I took note of the fact that Zeke had left the gun of the taller man on the floor next to him, and realized I wouldn't be able to hand over the gun of the shorter man because it had my prints on it, and I was considered a missing person. I'd make national news, and I couldn't have that.

The officer seemed to notice the gun too. "Was he the only one with a gun?" She asked.

"Yes," I lied coolly. Luckily, none of the other patrons heard the conversation and the hostess was still in the back. And since it was a mom and pop diner, there was no video surveillance.

The teenagers who had been taping the scene tried to sneak out and were ushered back in by the other officers. They huddled into a small group and pulled out their phones.

"Dude, we'll get in trouble if they see this stuff," one of them was saying in a hushed tone that only I could hear.

"We gotta get rid of it," the other said.

"Good thing I haven't posted mine yet." The third sighed with relief. "What about you guys?"

"Nope, I was waiting to get home to post it," the first said.

"Same here," the second replied.

I held back a relieved sigh.

"Ma'am, we're going to need statements from you and anyone else involved. Will you be available for questioning?" She asked.

I looked to see Zeke coming from the bathroom with Trace following behind him like a sullen child.

"I'll have to consult my boyfriend. We are very busy people."

She gave me a skeptical look, but shrugged. "That is understandable. We all lead very busy lives."

I motioned for her to wait, and rushed over to Zeke. In a barely audible voice, I said, "She wants to question us about the events that happened."

"We cannot do that. Why did you call them anyway?"

"To get the men put in prison. I said they tried to rob the place."

Zeke sighed, and pinched the bridge of his nose. "Kayla…"

"I told her we were very busy people, and that I'd need to consult you."

His hand dropped from his face, but his eyes remained closed. "I love you, but sometimes you can be a pain."

"I didn't know what else to do, and I wanted to call before someone else did."

"We could have brought them back for further questioning."

"In front of all these people? We'd be called kidnappers!" I fought to keep my voice low.

"You're the one who used your Magic. I disabled my opponent with use of brute force alone."

"He started it." I crossed my arms, pouting. "Plus, I guess I forgot that there were Humans here, in the heat of the moment."

He shook his head, and Trace spoke up. "How could you forget?"

"Well, mister 'I hide in bathrooms at the first signs of danger,' he shot fire at me. It kind of pissed me off."

The officer approached us just after I said this, and asked. "Have you finished consulting?"

"Yes," Zeke responded for me. "We will not be available for questioning. We must get home."

"What about you?" She asked, looking at Trace pointedly.

"I was in the bathroom the whole time," he said. "I didn't see anything."

She scowled, and relented. "I understand. You're free to go."

We nodded, and left the premises. Trace got in his little blue car, as we climbed into our red truck, and he followed us back to the house.

The drive was filled with a tense silence. I wished I was Ascended so I could see what was going on in Zeke's head, but that wouldn't come for a while yet. Instead, I resolved to continue practicing my Dragon Stone.

When we got home, Zeke got out of the truck, slamming the door shut. "Calling the cops…" He muttered as we approached the door, Trace following closely.

"I can tell you who they were," Trace said earnestly. "I caught a glimpse of them as we were leaving."

Zeke and I turned in unison. "Oh?" He asked.

"The man by the door was Alfonso, an' the man in the dining room was Edwin," Trace said. "They were set t'take the place of me and Don if anythin' ever happened to us. Which, anythin' did, so…" Trace trailed off.

"So they were, what, your understudies?" I asked.

"Somethin' like that," Trace said. He fidgeted.

"What is it?" I asked, taking in Trace's clearly uncomfortable body language.

"Well, I just," he sighed. "I don't know. I regret working for Xander. Had I known the full extent of what he was trying to do, I wouldn't have agreed to work for him in the first place."

"You may not have survived saying no, and in the end, you're doing the right thing," I said, trying to comfort him.

When Trace looked at me, his eyes were filled with mixed emotions. "You're right."

Zeke coughed, and said, "We should head inside."

I nodded and turned to the door. Trace began to move back toward his car.

"Trace, you are coming too," Zeke said. His voice commanded no refutations.

Trace stopped in his tracks, turning slowly

and following us to the house. Zeke shielded the keypad on the door, putting in the code and his print, and holding the door open for us.

We wasted no time getting inside, but didn't quite sprint through the door either. When Zeke shut the door behind us, there was a certain finality to it.

"We need to talk," he said.

Zeke was pacing. This wasn't good.

"Calling the cops could potentially draw attention to our species, let alone landing innocent Humans in danger." He turned to me. "We do *not* call the cops. Not now, not ever. Dragons have their own system for dealing with wrongdoers and traitors."

"Even with Humans around? One of them surely would have called the cops already," I asked.

"Then *let **them** do it*. You are not a Human anymore. You have not been for over a year now. It is time to stop thinking like a Human and start thinking like a Dragon."

"I've been a Human for most of my life up until this point," I balked. How could I stop thinking like one? It was as plain and natural to me as being a Dragon was to Zeke and Trace.

"Yet here you are, no longer a Human. Your responsibilities have grown, and you have grown. It is time to act like it." Zeke leaned against the doorframe, crossing his arms.

I blinked, "It's going to take some time, you know that, right?"

"You are picking up Dragon Magic faster than any other Dragon. You should pick up our habits too."

"You can't just expect me to change on a dime. I'm working on it, trust me."

Trace looked between us. "Am I really needed here? This is a bit of a lover's quarrel."

"Yes. I'm not done with you either." Zeke turned his cold gaze to Trace. "You say you want us to trust you, yet you went and hid in the bathroom at the first sign of trouble. How are we expected to let you into our clan if you cannot even stand a fight against your former allies?"

"I can't let them know I'm alive!" Trace exclaimed.

"Your presence will be discovered eventually. You cannot hide forever," Zeke almost growled.

Trace looked like a scolded child. Which was how I felt, at the moment. "I can try," he mumbled, scuffing his shoe along the edge of the rug.

"No. If you wish to prove your loyalty to our cause, you will show it. Hiding like a scared child will do nothing to prove yourself. The next time this happens, and there *will* be a next time, because we are at war, you will stand your ground and fight among us."

Trace was suddenly very interested in the toes of his boots. I glanced between him and Zeke, wondering what else Zeke had to say.

"I am finished here." Zeke turned and left the room, presumably to go to his office, leaving me and Trace alone in the entryway.

"He really went into us," Trace said, his southern drawl a little more pronounced than normal.

"Yeah. I've never seen him so pissed," I replied.

"You've never been on the receiving end of his anger. At least he spoke this time."

"Oh, no, I have been. He's scary when he's angry." The memory from our first major argument -- of cherry blossoms blooming on the walls, the floor cracking, and the lightbulb shattering -- resurfaced.

"The power of an Ascended. I can't even fathom it." Trace moved to sit in one of the chairs of the entry room.

"Nor can I, and I'm supposed to be one someday." I sat across from him, crossing one leg over the other.

"I've only mastered up to Scales. Can't imagine going much further."

"Maybe one day you'll get there," I said helpfully.

"If I live that long, perhaps." He let out a dry laugh.

"Oh, don't talk like that. Dragons can live up to thousands of years old. Look at Desmond and Molly. They're over 3,000 years old." I waved my hand arbitrarily in the air to articulate my point.

"Not Dragons who cross Xander, typically. And I've definitely done just that." I noticed that as he talked, Trace began bouncing his leg on the ball of his foot. This told me that talking about Xander made him anxious.

So I decided to change the subject.

"Hey, Trace?" I asked.

"Yeah?" He looked at me curiously.

"Why do you have a blue car?"

He blinked, perplexed. "'S my favorite color. Why do *you* have a red truck?"

"First of all, it's not *my* truck. It's Zeke's. And, secondly, I'm not sure why his truck is red."

"Maybe it's his favorite color?" Trace asked.

"It might be. There's a lot of red in this house."

"You've been dating him for months, an' you don't know his favorite color?"

"It hasn't exactly come up."

Trace shook his head. "There's always time for little things."

It was my turn to blink. "I guess you're right. Thanks, Trace."

With that, he stood up. "You're welcome, darlin'. I won't impose on you any longer. I'm gonna head out." As he neared the door, he spared me one last glance. "I hope the rest of your day is as beautiful as you are."

This brought an unwelcome heat to my cheeks and I waved him out the door. "Go, you schmooze."

He beamed at me, then left.

And just like that, I was alone with my thoughts.

I decided it was best to get my mind off of the day's events by going down to the training room. The long walk down the stairs didn't help my mood at all, and only focused my thoughts on the fact that Desmond and Molly were missing.

Trace had no idea where they were, and he couldn't risk bringing light to their disappearance to his contacts -- who weren't exactly trustworthy, from the sounds of it.

Zeke had practically shut down because of it.

I wasn't sure what to do or where to start looking for them. So I was going to do the only thing I knew how to do: Train.

I stripped off my flannel shirt, draping it over the back of the chair in the training room, then walked to the center of the room and sat in the middle of the floor. Placing my hands on my knees, and sitting up straight as I could, I closed my eyes. I meditated, focusing on the feeling of the Dragon Magic within me.

As I meditated, heat rose up around me. Peeking an eye open, I saw that I was sitting on a small stone island in the middle of a ring of magma. The heat rippled in the air, almost shimmering. Beads of sweat welled up and rolled down my body.

Taking a deep breath, I closed my eyes again, and focused again on the energy coursing through my veins. I willed the stone to close up, for the magma to recede back into the depths of the earth. The air around me cooled, and I began to shiver.

"Cool trick." I jumped at Zeke's voice. "Now the trick is to do it instantaneously."

"I thought you were doing paperwork?" I asked.

"I finished and wanted to see what you were up to." The ghost of a smile appeared on his lips. "Is that okay?"

"It's always okay." Standing, I approached him. I laced my fingers through his.

He placed a tender kiss to my lips, and I gladly drank him in.

"Would you like to spar with me?" I asked as we parted.

"Always the romantic." He chuckled, and began to unbutton his shirt. He folded it onto the seat of the same chair my shirt was on, and followed me into the center of the room.

Facing each other, we fell into our stances. Zeke was the first to move, and it was in this moment that I realized he was not going to be pulling any punches today.

He blasted through the wall of rock that I pulled up, shattering it to dust. I barely had time to pull up my arms to block the punch, loaded with ice. I brought forth my fire, melting the ice, but still stumbling back from the force of the hit.

I regained my ground, ducking low to sweep his feet out from under him. A surge of air lifted him up, higher than my leg, and he was suddenly behind me.

His arms wrapped around me, not as an embrace but as a grapple, and I struggled to drop my weight. I couldn't turn, and his hold was too strong.

"Uncle. Uncle! I surrender!" I yelped.

"You win this time!"

I felt him grinning against my ear. "I could not let you get too cocky. You may be the Blood Dragon, but you still have a lot to learn."

"I feel like there's more to it than that. Normally you build up to kicking my ass." I rubbed my arms where his punch had collided with them, checking for bruising.

He thought for a moment. "No, no ulterior motive."

"You sure you're not pissed about Xander's people interrupting our breakfast, or Trace hiding, or me using my abilities in front of Humans, or Desmond and Molly--"

"Enough." Zeke turned coldly, grabbing his shirt from the chair and putting it on. He left me alone and confused in the training area.

So I sat down to meditate again.

Learn more about the series:

Blood Dragon: The Search Begins takes place in the *Dragon's Ascent* series, specifically within the pages of the first book, Dragon's Ascent: Blood Dragon. *Dragon's Ascent* is told from the point of view of Kayla Cochikev, a woman-turned-Dragon who has been chosen by the Gods to stop the Great Undoing, an act that would bring an untimely end to the world. Initially, she has some trouble fitting into her new role as the Blood Dragon, but with the help of her mentor and partner, Zeke, she finds her footing and embarks on the task of training her newfound abilities to defeat the leader of the Dragon Mafia and keep the world safe from harm. Dragon's Ascent: Blood Dragon, the first of an urban fantasy series, is still in the process of being edited. Be sure to look for news on its release date to learn more about Kayla and Zeke's journey.

You Win, You Lose
Written by: Ben Oneal

Chapter 1

    He let the contestants watch as he spun the wheel. It was more than satisfying to see their reactions to which body part was next to go. Each sliver of the pie ranged from something as small as a little piggy, to an arm or a leg. One slice even called for death. Only one time since he began the game, had some lucky contestant landed on death. To be sure, most wish they had landed on a quick end to the intense pain that multiple spins promised.

    Tricia Van Ness, the eighteenth contestant, had been lucky on her first two spins. Only if you could call losing her index finger on her right hand, and her big toe on her left foot lucky. Even though the game show host had done nothing to stop the blood pouring from her wounds, the flow was down to a trickle due to the body's natural clotting effect.

Her screams went unnoticed for two very good reasons. First, the killer lived a half a mile from his nearest neighbor. Second, even if his neighbors were as close as next door, the soundproofing he had installed insured no sound would escape the confines of his game room.

"Please stop, I beg you, please," Tricia pleaded. The pain from her hand and foot was excruciating.

"Why? We've just started," The Host said cheerfully.

She believed that he must be smiling, but her captor wore a Kim Jong Un mask; hiding any chance of her knowing who he might be.

"Please let me go." She was sobbing hard, as the host spun the wheel.

"You're doing really well Tricia. Remember

if you survive five spins, you will be free."

The flapper clicked away as each nail spun around the perimeter of the wheel. Both contestant and host studied the wheel, as the friction of the downward pointing arrow slowed this spin with the passing of each metal post. Tricia watched the prize wheel with growing dread. Click, click, click, click, click …click, ….click, ……click.

"Nooooooo!" Tricia cried.

"Whaaaat? Tricia, you are one lucky girl," The Host said, sounding as if he was really happy for her.

The wheel had landed on right hand thumb. The Host wasted no time; he walked over to the table, and grabbed the loppers.

"Are you ready my dear?" The Host asked, as he turned back toward her.

"No! Please, no more," Tricia cried.

The Host tried to position the loppers to cut off her thumb, but she struggled against him so much that he had to stop for a second.

"Tricia, Tricia, Tricia, if you don't let me cut off your thumb, I will just cut off your arm."

This somehow seemed to break into Trisha's fear racked mind. She reluctantly stopped resisting, turned away, and cried hard as he positioned the loppers on her thumb. Her screams were like music to the host's ears, but not as pleasing as the crunch of the loppers cutting through the bone and cartilage of her thumb.

"Two more like this and you will be free. Did you hear me Tricia? Free."

Tricia was beyond hearing. She was in more pain than she had ever experienced in her life. Never mind that she no longer had a digit to oppose the three fingers that remained on her right hand. If she survived two more rounds, and she was given her freedom, she decided she would somehow find a way to go on.

Most of the contestants that came before her had already lost an arm, or a leg, or even their head at this stage of the game. Death came quickly for them after that, but angels must be watching over her, because her next two spins resulted in the loss of another toe on her left foot, and a middle finger on her left hand.

"My, my, my, Tricia. You are the first contestant to survive all five rounds. That is quite remarkable." The host sounded truly impressed.

Through the pain and tears, Tricia found her voice. "Now let me go, please."

"Like I promised Tricia, since you survived five rounds, you will be free," he said.

He walked over to the table that sat on the right side of the room. It was the table where he kept his special tools. He stood there for a moment, surveying the tools of the game. He smiled under his mask, and reached for the hunting knife. He turned toward her, and with his back to the camera, he lifted the mask, revealing his face to her for the first time since he had taken her. He was holding the knife menacingly.

Even though the pain from her hands and feet tore at her soul, two questions forced their way into her mind. *Why is he holding the knife? If he is letting me go, why is he showing me his face?*

"Are you ready to die, my dear?" The Host asked.

"What? You promised me I would go free."

"No, I said you would be free. I never said I would let you go," The Host said, and began to laugh. It was an overboard laugh, like from a person who is socially awkward; which was exactly what he was, awkward.

Now it was time to end the game. As Tricia screamed, and struggled to free herself, the host held the knife to her heart. He looked into her eyes, the back of his hand rubbed against her breast; he paused, and thought for a moment. He sat the knife down, and began to unbutton her top.

Once he exposed her, he thrilled at the sight of her. The host started to think it might be nice to have a little fun before he killed her. He reached out and touched her with the tips of his fingers. It was clear that his touch repulsed her.

"You are a sick bastard!" she screamed.

Unfortunately, those were almost the same words that Alison Meyers, the first girl he attempted to love, used on that fateful night so long ago. When he failed to perform, he discovered that he was set up by Alison and her boyfriend. That's when she said those words; "You are a sick fuck!" She began to laugh. The memory ripped away at his sanity.

He backed away, grabbed the knife, and began to stab her feverishly. He finally stopped long after she passed from this world. There were so many wounds, that her chest was unrecognizable. His arm was so tired that he could barely hold the knife.

"I'm not a sick fuck Alison; I'm not a sick fuck." He sat back on his heels, and cried. To The Host, Tricia Van Ness, was no longer there.

Because of the way this episode ended, he did not feel like closing the show with his usual ending. Instead he pressed the remote, and the screen went black.

Chapter 2

Before he was The Host, the star of the show was known only as Gerald Spurling. Gerald had killed two other people before finding his muse. They had given him that release that he desired. To kill was the answer to a question that he had lived with for his first seventeen years of life. One that was left unanswered, until that one glorious day, where a chance meeting with a homeless man, changed his life forever. Although he tried hard to think about it, he couldn't remember why he chose this man, besides being in the wrong place at the right time.

He followed the homeless man into the alley and beat him to death with a piece of pipe he found. With each crushing blow of the pipe, a deep desire awoke within his soul. The feeling was so intense, so wonderful that if he would have been caught right then and there, he would have felt satisfied that he had fulfilled his purpose in life.

He made his way home filled with immense satisfaction. He lay in bed unable to sleep. He was sure that at any time there would be police knocking at his door. That knock never came. As the days, then weeks passed his fear of answering for the life he took melted away. There was however, a new desire that began to occupy his thoughts; the need to kill again.

His second kill was someone that he knew, and it was personal. His mother was not a good mother by any sense of the word, but despite her lack of parenting skills, he loved her completely. He had never known his dad, and found little male connections with the men his mom brought home. One of these men that stayed with them for a while, was a man named Jesse Staten. He was an abusive drunk, and regularly hit his mom. She made all the usual excuses for why she might deserve this treatment, but none satisfied Gerald.

    At a very young age, Jesse had made bullying a life choice. As it was with most all bullies, when someone was smaller or weaker, he did his best to intimidate, demean, and physically abuse, but if he was confronted by someone who was bigger or stronger, he was not so aggressive. Unless he was drunk, then all bets were off. During those times, he often woke up the next day with bruises or a black eye that he couldn't explain.

    Almost four months after Gerald beat the homeless man to death, his desire, no his need to kill manifested itself in a most useful way. As he came in through the back fence, he noticed that Jesse was working on his Harley in the garage, with Thunderstruck by AC/DC blasting from the speakers that sat on his work bench. Gerald entered unnoticed. He found a thirteen and half inch long Craftsman box wrench. It felt good in his hand. He crept up to Jesse, and cleared his throat. When Jesse turned with that sour look that Gerald had seen a thousand times, he swung the wrench, and connected with Jesse's throat. He wasn't sure of the anatomy of the throat, but the satisfying crunch that transcended the loud music was magical.

The bully fell onto his back, grasping at his throat.

"Not so fucking tuff now, are you?" Gerald said, breathing hard.

Jesse mouthed the words that would never come. The fear in his eyes was all that mattered to Gerald. It spoke volumes.

"Now it is time to die, you son of a bitch!" Visions of the abuse his mom suffered at Jesse's hands came into his mind. Gerald raised the wrench, and smashed it into Jesse's head, again and again. He didn't stop until the face was no more.

He raised his fist into the air, and looked as if he might howl like a werewolf after killing its prey, but the howl did not come. What came was a sense of great fulfillment washing over his soul. "Damn! That felt good," he hissed, as rivulets of Jesse's blood coursed down his face.

As the sense of euphoria wore away, the killer realized that he had a situation that was not there in the first kill. He had to get rid of the body. He just left the homeless man in the alley, for anyone to find, but there was a connection to his mom, that might be traced back to him.

This was his first experience with cutting up a body. He cut the legs, arms, and what was left of Jesse's head off using a very sharp hunting knife, and a hammer and chisel to break through the bones. Once he was done, he looked around the garage, found an old tarp, and began to wrap Jesse up for disposal.

He put Jesse's body in the trunk of his car, and drove him to a spot near the Chain O' Lakes State Park. He dragged him into the woods, and quickly dug a shallow grave. After filling in the dirt, he covered the grave with leaves and branches. This was not a place that people would ever be, unless they were cutting a new path through the woods.

Once he got home, he rode Jesse's Harley into downtown Fort Wayne, and left it for someone to take. After he returned home, he cleaned the garage. Then he gathered anything that was connected to Jesse, like clothes and other personal items, and put them in a Goodwill donation box in Auburn just twenty miles up I-69. Again he was blessed, and was never caught.

Chapter 3

Once Jesse was gone, Gerald somehow convinced his mother to clean up her act. She started to attend AA meetings, found a job at Wendy's, and met a man that Gerald actually liked a lot. Gerald promised his mom that he would finish college, and make a good life for himself. With the help of scholarships he was able to get almost a full ride to Ball State University, majoring in Computer Technology. He also got a minor in Telecommunications. Gerald put all his efforts into graduating, finding a good job, and would not kill again until after he had fulfilled his promise.

He soon found a job at the General Motors Truck Assembly plant in Fort Wayne. As the paychecks came rolling in, he was able to buy an old farm house, northeast of Columbia City, thirty minutes from Fort Wayne, and far away from the nearest neighbor to afford him a little privacy.

He had done as he promised his mother. He had gone to college, and made a life for himself. Now it was time to follow his dreams. His new mission in life came to him as an epiphany as he worked through his minor in Telecommunications. One evening, as he ate dinner at the dorm, a game show that involved a prize wheel came on the television in the cafeteria. As he watched the contestants spin the wheel, a whimsical thought crossed his mind. *What if with each spin of the wheel that the contestant lost something, instead of winning a prize? What if what they lost was a body part?* He asked himself.

From that moment on, even though his dream would have to wait until he had the means and the location, his path in life was set. He learned everything that he could about film making, editing, and bringing to life a final product worthy of an Emmy. When he had the money he required, and the place, he worked night and day to bring it to fruition.

The farm had an out building that had been built just a year before the previous owner died. For the next six months, he laboriously sound proofed, set up lighting, and built the set for his show. At the same time he scoured the internet for used studio cameras and editing equipment. Once he had everything he needed to fulfill his dream, he made a visit to the David Letterman Communication and Media Building at Ball State. He needed to talk to Joey Terrell, a once-fellow student, now an Associate Professor in the Telecommunications program, to help him set it up.

Out of curiosity more than anything else, Terrell agreed to help him with the final touches. It was Friday, so they agreed to meet in Fort Wayne, on Saturday. They met at the McDonalds, just off I-69. They took Gerald's car, and drove west on US-30. Thirty minutes later, Gerald turned into the driveway of the farmhouse.

With pride Gerald walked Terrell through the studio. Terrell was impressed by the set up and the equipment that his old school mate put together.

"Ready to get to work?" Gerald asked.

"Let's do it." It was clear that Terrell was excited.

They set up the cameras, so Gerald could remote control them from a single device. By the afternoon, they were almost finished. Gerald went to the farmhouse to get them sandwiches and a couple of beers. While Gerald was gone, Terrell had been wondering about something that had dominated his thoughts. There was something on the set that was covered by a gray tarp, and Terrell decided to check it out. He peaked under the cover, and it only served to add to his wonder. At that moment, Gerald walked in.

"What the hell are you doing?" Gerald was clearly surprised by his trespass.

"I was wondering what was under the tarp. Sorry, I guess my curiosity got the best of me," Terrell said feeling a little embarrassed.

"I wish you would've asked," Gerald said shaking his head.

"Sorry!" Terrell said, but he had something else on his mind. "What's this?" He pointed to the tarp.

"It was none of your business," Gerald said, continuing his head shake.

"But why does this prize wheel have body parts as prizes. One prize even said death? I don't understand." Terrell was clearly confused.

"That's right, you don't understand. Here,

help me remove the tarp, and I will explain."

When Terrell turned to remove the tarp, Gerald hit him with the same box wrench he used to beat Jesse to death. A while later, when Terrell came to, he was strapped to a chair that now sat in the middle of the stage. His head hurt terribly. His eyes focused on the space around him. The tarp had been removed, to reveal Gerald's prize wheel in all its glory.

"Gerald, what the hell is going on? Why am I in this chair?" Intense fear was creeping into his mind.

"Well, I never intended to for you to be my first contestant, but here we are," Gerald explained.

"Contestant? What are you talking about?"

"This is my game show, and like I said, you are my first contestant. Unfortunately, I will have to gag you to keep you from revealing my name." He placed a gag in his mouth. "Let's get started."

He positioned the cameras, did a quick sound check, and cued the music. Finally, he pulled on an Albert Einstein mask, and activated the cameras.

"Hello, I am your Host...." And that is how it began.

Chapter 4

"What's going on, you gorgeous lump of man muscle?" I asked my boss, after I made sure the door was shut. I am Special Agent Benjamin Kroh of the Behavioral Analysis Unit of the FBI, and Noah Bennett is my best friend and boss.

"Sit down, puny human. Kroh, we have a bad one," Noah said.

"Really?"

"Oh yeah." I could see that something was eating at him.

"Tell me what's on your mind." I was serious now.

"Some hikers at the Chain O' Lakes State Park in Indiana, happened upon a body dump. They alerted the DNR, and the DNR quickly realized that they were in over their heads. They called the Sheriff's Department."

"How many we got?"

"Eleven so far, but it's hard to tell, there are varying degrees of body parts missing."

"No shit!"

"Yes shit. This guy has been dumping bodies there for quite awhile."

"How long?"

"At least ten years. Once the body count hit five, they called us, and asked for help."

"Are you giving this to me?" I asked.

"Well, I didn't ask you here to look at your ugly ass face."

"Oh Noah, you really love me. You really, really love me." I faked some happy tears.

"Get the hell out of here fool," Noah said as he looked down at his file and smirked.

"Love you too, Noah," I said, as I opened

the door, and hurried out.

I called my team, Zindzhi Cole and Martin Owens. Zindzhi, or Zee as she preferred, is one of the best agents I know, and Marty is my Navajo computer genius. As I was filling Zee in on the case, Marty walked in, already researching what they knew about the Chain O' Lakes murders.

"I wish you'd wait until I told you we were on a case before you started researching it," I said feigning anger.

"I'm sorry sir, but if I waited for you, we may never solve the case."

"He's right, you know," Zee said shrugging.

"Whaaaat?" I said, this time feigning hurt. "You know that would really hurt, if it wasn't so true."

Zee and Marty high-fived, and we all had a laugh.

"Seriously we need to get moving on this quick. So far, they have found eleven bodies at the dump site. A couple of bodies have been there for quite a while, maybe ten years or more, but some are quite recent. One body they found was of a woman who was reported missing only two weeks ago. She has been identified as Tricia Van Ness, a twenty-seven-year-old mother of three. She was last seen at the Half-Price Books on Coliseum Boulevard in Fort Wayne, Indiana. They found her car in the book store parking lot," I told them.

"Another girl was preliminarily identified as Janice Hunter. She went missing almost two months ago. She was last seen at a Kroger grocery store in Columbia City," Marty added.

"Less than two months; wow!" Zee said.

"I see here that they were both missing body parts." Marty said.

"Van Ness was missing three fingers and two toes. Janice Hunter was missing her left hand, her right arm, and her right leg."

"What about the others? Were they missing body parts?"

"Of the bodies they have found so far, everyone was missing some body parts. It seems to be random. No two bodies have the same missing parts," I told them. "Marty, I need two things; airline tickets and a connection between our victims. Zee I need you to head home and pack your travel bag. I will call you as soon as I find out when we leave."

Three hours later Zee and I were in the air, and heading to Fort Wayne International Airport. Since the BAU does not have a jet at their disposal, like the agents on the television show Criminal Minds, we are forced to fly coach. It would be at least four hours before we could get to Fort Wayne, so Zee and I went over everything that we had so far. That gave our friend, Agent Vernon, time to drive up from Indianapolis. He had already been in touch with the local authorities, and filled us in as we left the terminal. Since we were incommunicado during the flight, the info that Marty had found during that time downloaded to our tablets as soon as we landed.

As we drove toward the dump site in the Chain O' Lakes State Park, we studied the new data. In the time we traveled from Washington, two more bodies had been found. All the bodies found so far, except for one, were buried with some form of identification, but it would be a while before these could be authenticated. Every name had been matched to a missing person's case in or around northern Indiana.

As we pulled up to the dump site, I was happy to see one of my favorite people. Paul Meacham, the Indy field office forensics specialist, was already on the scene. He was instrumental in the capture of both the Fingertip Killer, and the Guardian of I-69. He is tall, thin, and a master of lame jokes, but as far as doing his job, I couldn't ask for more. Vernon walked us over to a group of men standing around a Noble County cruiser.

"Sheriff Maxwell, I would like you to meet Special Agent Benjamin Kroh and Special Agent

Zindzhi Cole."

"Glad to meet you both. I've heard a lot about you, Agent Kroh."

"I'm glad to meet you sir, and please just call me Kroh."

"You are pretty famous around Indiana; with the Fingertip Killer and the Guardian. Hope you're as good as everyone says you are."

"My team makes me look good sir. Without them I'm just another Agent."

"I can't say that I'm unhappy to let you take the lead," Sheriff Maxwell said with a smile.

"Please Sheriff Maxwell, I would much rather work together. Besides, you know the area and the people around here. Working together will be the best way to catch this guy."

"I'll help you in any way I can. So you're sure it's a male suspect?" The Sheriff asked.

"Yes sir. Although I cannot rule out a female, males are statistically more likely."

We talked for a while longer, and I found that I liked the Sheriff from the start. He walked me through the dump site, showing me where each body was buried and their preliminary identification.

"We got another one over here," someone yelled from about fifty yards to my left.

We walked that way, and the forensics team pointed to the skull that they had uncovered.

"Damn! That's fourteen," Sheriff Maxwell said as he pulled off his Stetson and wiped the sweat from his forehead.

"The way this area is laid out, I have a feeling that we have more," I said shaking my head.

"Sheriff Maxwell, where's the coroner?" Zee asked.

"He's the guy in the green over there." The Sheriff pointed to his left.

As Zee and Vernon went over to talk to the coroner, I spent a few more minutes with the Sheriff. I could see that he was taking responsibility for every death.

"I should've realized something was going on; fourteen bodies, I should've seen it."

"These guys spend their lives hiding their true nature. If it weren't for the chance encounter of the hikers cutting across an area with no trails, we may have never found them. I'll bet that very few are from your jurisdiction. There is no way you could have known."

"I know you're right, but…"

"Let's just catch this guy, Sheriff," I said as I put my hand on his shoulder.

Chapter 5

Over the next couple of days they uncovered five more bodies. That brought the total body count to nineteen. All but two had some form of identification left with the body. Three coroners from surrounding counties volunteered to assist with the autopsies. Although DNA would ultimately ensure their identification, it was fairly certain that we knew who our victims were. They all matched missing person cases going back at least ten years.

The ages of the victims ranged from fourteen to sixty-eight. Sex or ethnicity didn't seem to factor into the killer's choice, because those factors were all over the place. The two cases that interested me most were two of the oldest cases. Their bodies had no identification left with the bodies.

"Our killer seemed to have purposely left identification with all the bodies but two. Either he hadn't found his M.O. yet, or these bodies hold the secret to his discovery," I told Zee and Vernon, as I bit into my Kraut dog, at Jeff's Coney, on E. State Blvd., in Fort Wayne. For a moment I got lost in the taste of the perfectly steamed bun, as it mixed with the sauerkraut and hot dog.

"Earth to Kroh," Zee broke into my thoughts.

"Sorry! I just feel that unless we can find an eyewitness or video evidence that leads us to a suspect in the taking of the people we have identified, our best chance of finding our killer is with the two unidentified people," I said as I washed down my last bite with an ice cold Triple XXX Root Beer.

"We've still got Marty. If there is a connection, he'll find it," Vernon said.

"Even as great as Marty is, I fear he will find nothing, because I bet there is nothing. I feel very strongly that every one of the known victims were random; victims of opportunity and chance," I offered.

"I agree," Zee chimed in. "I believe that the only chance of finding our killer, lies with the identification of the two unknowns."

Vernon got on the phone, and relayed our concerns to the Sheriff. He asked him to talk to the coroners involved in the autopsies of our two unknowns, and relay our concerns to them. At the same time I called Meacham, and told him to re-examine the two unknown victim's gravesites. I knew it was a long shot, because Meacham is one of the best crime scene techs I've ever worked with. The chances of him missing anything, is next to none.

Another thing that we now had to deal with, were the multitude of reporters, and news vans parked along the road outside the Chain O' Lakes State Park, near the dump site. I had hoped that we could forgo the pleasure of the media circus for a while longer, but such is life.

*****

Gerald Spurling sat watching the news with both anger and excitement manifesting in his thoughts. He was mad about losing his precious collection. He had spent many glorious hours conversing with the contestants, and introducing each new member to the group. Now as he watched the authorities desecrating his shrine to the game, his thoughts grew dark.

His anger was tempered by something new. *Maybe it is time to share my game with the rest of the world.* As this thought pushed its way into his mind, the light of new possibilities brightened his thoughts. *Yes, this could be interesting.* There was much work that needed to be done, and it needed to be done soon. Riding the media wave that started with the discovery of his shrine would certainly boost the hunger for the wonderful nourishment that only he could provide.

*****

"Hey Kroh, I got some bad news," Marty, my super geek, said as I answered the phone.

"What's up Marty?" I really dreaded it whenever he said bad news.

"It looks like your un-sub has decided to go public. He's taking the Guardian route, and is showing videos on the Internet."

The Guardian was killing child molesters, and leaving them along I-69. To give his murders justification, he displayed videos of their crimes against children on the Internet. Now it seems our new un-sub was doing the same.

"How bad is it Marty?" I asked not really wanting his answer.

"It's a game show, Kroh. You have to see it for yourself. I sent you a link."

"Thanks Marty. While I'm checking this out, see what you can do about shutting it down," I said as I hung up, and clicked on the link.

The first thing that came up was a reasonably professional opening to a game show, with an announcer using the universal cadence to most every game show opening.

"Welcome to the newest and greatest game show in the world…

You Win, You Lose!"

Strange as it may seem, a man came on wearing an Einstein mask. He first introduced himself as, The Host. And then he introduced a person sitting bound to a chair as Contestant #1.

The contestant clearly had something stuffed in his mouth, and was unable to speak. Then the scene zoomed out revealing a professional looking set, with a big prize wheel sitting center stage.

The Host walked up to the wheel, and with a flourish, gave a quick description of the prizes on the wheel. He finished with describing the smallest prize sliver on the wheel as death.

"Believe me; the contestant will be hoping to land on this prize, if he is unlucky enough to miss it during his first couple of spins. Let's get started."

The Host grabbed the wheel, and spun it hard. The flapper clicked against each metal post as it went by. Click, click, click, click, click, …click, ….click, ……click. Finally it slowed, until it stopped.

"Left foot!" The Host announced, as there was a close-up of the arrow shaped flapper pointing between two metal posts at a sliver of the board that said left foot. The host wasted no time, promptly walking off camera, and then came back carrying a large set of loppers. The camera followed him as he walked over to the contestant. The contestant began to struggle feverishly against the straps that held him in place.

On the top left corner of the screen was a heart monitor, and his already fast heart rate rose significantly as The Host came closer.

Undeterred by the muffled begging, or the struggle to get away, The Host placed the blades of the lopper around the contestant's ankle, and cut off his foot. Our un-sub must have placed microphones near the contestant, because the sound of the loppers cutting through the bone came across loud and clear. I felt the bile rise in my throat.

Zee and I both wanted to look away, but forced ourselves to watch the macabre spectacle. The contestant's begging changed to a muffled scream of pain. I found myself rubbing my reattached finger that the Fingertip Killer had cut off a few years before. That made what I was watching so much more real to me. The host again wasted no time, turned, and walked back to the wheel.

"Spin number two!" The Host chimed.

The next spin cost the contestant his right hand thumb. As gruesome as this was, the third spin was fatal. As the wheel completed its spin, the prize, if you could call it that, was death.

"Well isn't that disappointing? Two more spins, and you would've been free." The Host, wearing the smiling Einstein mask, walked up to the struggling contestant, and as the camera zoomed in for a close-up, he pushed a hunting knife into the poor man's heart.

The contestant's eyes glared at The Host, as he attempted to speak into the gag. Then his eyes gradually closed, and his head slowly dropped to his chest.

"Well, tune in next time for another exciting episode of…

You Win, You Lose!"

From this point on, every day, a new episode of the game show made its way onto the Internet. I refused to watch the episode with the fourteen-year-old boy. I just couldn't.

Chapter 6

Four days into the investigation, and our only hope seemed to be the two oldest unidentified bodies found at the dump site. The first of the two unknowns was a mess, his skull was in fragments. It was clear that he was beaten severely about the head. Finding all the skull fragments and the teeth was a losing process. There were no fingerprints, due to the length of time since the body was dumped. The only hope might be dental records, but from the condition of the teeth they had found, it didn't look as though the victim had ever been in the vicinity of a dentist.

The second unknown gave us more hope. There was nothing left except bones, a skull, and a complete set of teeth. That at least gave us hope of a dental match. Marty had already started a search of missing persons, using the estimates of height and how long since the person had died.

Since all but two of the victims were from northeastern Indiana, Marty concentrated his search to those areas first. He started with a forty-five mile radius from the Chain O' Lakes dump site. This would encompass Fort Wayne, where ten of the victims were taken. This search came up with eight missing persons, five were children, two were adult women, and only one was an adult male. Unfortunately, he was much too old to fit our profile. Marty called to update me on his search.

"Kroh, I'm wondering if maybe the two male victims were transients, and never reported missing," Marty offered.

"Just keep checking my friend. I have no

doubt that if the identity of our victim is out there you will find him. If he is a transient, we'll just find another way to catch this guy."

While Zee and I sat there talking to him, he expanded the search to a ninety mile radius. This search resulted in seventeen more missing persons. Again, most of the missing were children; twelve juveniles, three adult women, and two adult men.

"Kroh, I just got a hit on two males, both match age and height ranges. They are Jeremy Robert Smith from South Bend, Indiana, and Joseph Stephen Terrell from Muncie, Indiana. Smith was a Deputy Prosecutor in South Bend. He disappeared ten years ago."

"Could be somebody he helped put away," Zee offered.

"That's very possible. The other guy, Terrell, was an Associate Professor in the Telecommunications program at Ball State University," Marty added.

"What?" I asked, feeling a tingle in my gut.

"Do you think there's a connection?" Marty asked.

"I don't know, but it sounds promising. Get more background on both of them, but concentrate on Terrell."

"You got it boss," Marty replied.

"Good job, Marty," Zee said.

"Thanks, Marty," I said, then called Sheriff Maxwell, and updated him on what we found.

"Are you getting that gut feeling?" Zee asked.

"Yes, I am. Looking at the quality of the filming of 'You Win, You Lose', it is evident that the person had knowledge of the craft. It just seems right," I said rubbing my reattached finger.

Marty called a few moments later.

"Kroh, like I said, Joseph Terrell was an Associate Professor of Telecommunications at Ball State. He went missing 11 years ago. Last time anyone saw him was after he taught his last class on a Friday, and did not show for a scheduled meeting on Saturday morning. I have asked the local authorities for a copy of his dental records, and when I told them what we were looking into, they promised to get back as soon as possible. What do you think?" Marty asked.

"Road trip?" Zee asked.

"Road trip," I responded. "Thanks again, Marty."

I called Crystal Markum, a detective with the Anderson Police Department, and the love of my life, hoping she could meet us in Muncie. She said she could, and that she would meet us at the Muncie Police Department. Once we arrived, we would gather everything they had on Terrell. Thanks to Crystal, it was waiting for us, tied in a bow.

Next, we hurried to the Ball Communication building at Ball State University. We met with Owen Jarvis, the Interim Chair of the Department of Telecommunications. At our request, he gathered some people who had worked alongside Terrell, and some of those were also classmates. I found one of the least disturbing pictures of the game show that we had watched.

"I want to show you something, but I must warn you that it is quite disturbing." I slid the picture across a desk. Judy Warner, an Assistant Professor who had worked closely with Terrell, gasped.

"That's Joey!" She started to cry.

"I'm sorry, but we had to know. There is something else that we need to know. Was there anyone that you can remember that might've had something against Terrell?"

"No way," was the unanimous response.

"Wait a minute," Judy Warner said. "I seem to remember a guy who hung around Terrell, he seemed a little different, or maybe awkward is a better term."

"Are you talking about Game Boy?" Jarvis asked.

"Game Boy?" Zee asked.

"Yes, Terrell was one of the only people

who got along with him. The reason we call him Game Boy, was because he really liked the "Wheel of Fortune."

"Son of a Bitch! What was his name?" I asked urgently.

"Oh my…huh…Ster…Sterling, no Spurling. I'm not sure of the first name, but I'm really sure of the last name," Judy said.

"Yeah. She's right," The others chimed in.

"Is it possible for us to get more information on Spurling?" I asked.

"I should have his information, I'll be right back." The interim chair stood, and walked out of the room.

Ten minutes later he was back with the name, Gerald Spurling. "I'm sure if you check with the Administration Office you can find out a lot more."

On the way back north, Zee shot Marty the name and birth date of Spurling. A few minutes later I got a call from Marty.

"What do you know Navajo?" I asked, and

got a look from Zee.

"I got the mother load… White man. You got a lot of the usual stuff that I will give you in a moment. But there's something I think you'd like to know first. He owns a farm near Mongo, Indiana. It's about thirty miles from the dump site. I sent you the coordinates."

I called ahead and told Sheriff Maxwell what we had found, but cautioned him not to spook Spurling. I suggested that he should do a drive-by in an unmarked vehicle.

We really didn't know what to expect. There was not a lot of info on Spurling. We contacted the truck assembly plant where he worked, and found out that he had been on vacation for two weeks. That was about the same time the news reported the discovery of the dump site. Spurling's supervisor told our agent that Spurling was a bit of an odd duck. He kept mostly to himself, and tended to make the people he worked around a little uncomfortable. He has also been called into HR a few times for inappropriate conduct. The note in the file indicated that the HR rep didn't believe that it was intentional, it was just him. The HR rep wrote that he thought Spurling might have some kind of an empathy disorder. He just lacks the ability to care about the feelings of others. As we did with the people at Ball State, we cautioned them not to talk to anyone about Terrell or Spurling.

I called Sheriff Maxwell again to have some deputies stake out the property. Although I had already looked at the property on Google Earth, it was best to have eyes on the property from the ground.

We met at the Sheriff's office in Albion. As we sat in their conference room we got word that Spurling had left the house, and gone to the outbuilding. With the aerial view on Google Map, we planned our next move. We decided that Deputy Virgil Evans and I would come in from the front, and Zee and Agent Vernon, would enter from the back. We had more agents and deputies surrounding the property just in case he decided to run.

As we arrived at Spurling's property, we were informed that he had not left the outbuilding. As we moved into position, our Agents moved to clear his house. When I reached the front door of the outbuilding, I quietly checked the door, and it was locked. I radioed the team in back, and coordinated our entry.

"Go!"

Two deputies simultaneously hit the doors with Blackhawk Dynamic Entry Rams, and the doors splintered inward. We entered the building, guns first. I took the left, deputy Evans took the right. It was evident that Spurling knew we were coming, because the building was dark. While I kept watch, Evans found the lights.

The room in front of us was the set from the game show from the videos. There in the middle of the set was a chair. Thoughts of the time I was strapped to a chair while a crazy bastard shot me, and cut off my finger raced through my head. I forced those thoughts from my mind, and continued to scope out the room.

Suddenly, from a dark hallway to the left, a figure in an Einstein mask came at us fast, as a scream came from every speaker in the building. My mind went into overdrive. From the corner of my eye I saw Evans raise his gun, but my gut told me that something was off. I raised my arm just in time to deflect his shot. I wrapped my arms around Einstein as he fell into my arms.

I quickly pushed Einstein to the floor as unintelligible mumblings came from under the mask. I quickly realized as I began to handcuff Einstein that the arms hanging down at his sides were not real. As Deputy Evans held the gun on our suspect, I pulled off the mask. It was not Spurling.

I looked up at Evans, and I could tell that he was feeling the effects of almost shooting an innocent person.

"Don't worry, nothing happened here. Okay? Let's find Spurling," I said, and he shook his head.

We pulled the unknown person outside the door, and radioed for someone to grab him. We reentered the building, and quickly cleared the game show set. Zee and Vernon entered the room shaking their heads. We started going room to room, looking for any place Spurling might be.

I found the door to the basement, and Vernon and I slowly descended the steps. Once we reached the bottom, I noticed a metal door, with the words 'Film Vault', written in red. After making sure that there was no place he could be hiding in the rest of the basement, we headed for the metal door.

"FBI!" I yelled as I banged on the door. "Come out, with your hands up, and you won't be hurt."

We stood on both sides the door, and waited, hoping that he might come out. After a few moments, we knew if he was in there he wasn't coming out voluntarily. I tried the door, and it was unlocked. I swung the door open, and chanced a look inside the room. There were rows of shelves on both sides of the room containing film canisters.

I entered the room, ready for anything. As we proceeded carefully, checking each row of shelves, the left group of shelves fell toward us like a stack of dominoes. Vernon was trapped under the landslide of falling shelves.

"Vernon?" I asked, hoping he was okay.

I had no time to think about him, because Spurling came out from behind the only standing shelf on the left. He was holding a film canister over his head, and running at me screaming at the top of his lungs. It was clear that he was about to bash my head in. I launched myself at Spurling, and caught him waist high, knocking him backwards. The film canister was knocked from his hands, and landed on my lower back.

The pain was excruciating, but when I felt Spurling crab walking backward, I fought through the pain and scrambled after him. That's when I felt the knife cut across my palm. Spurling got to his knees, raised the knife in both hands, and I knew I was helpless to stop him from stabbing me in the back.

A shot rang out, and Spurling was knocked backward against the wall, eyes wide with shock, and was dead a moment later.

"Are you okay?" Zee asked, sounding worried.

"My back hurts like a son of a bitch, and the bastard about sliced my hand in half." I held it up, and Zee found a roll of paper towels.

"Here put this in your hand, and make a fist," Zee said.

Suddenly my thoughts turned to Vernon. "Vernon. He's under those shelves."

I winced as I got up, but I wasn't going to let that bother me. Evans had radioed that we had the suspect, and that we needed help down in the basement. The shelves were heavy, so it was a good thing that the Sheriff along with the other Agents on the scene came into the room.

We quickly moved each shelf one at a time, until we found Vernon. He was conscious, and it was clear he was hurting.

*****

The man in the Einstein mask, who would've been contestant number twenty, was a young college student from Fort Wayne, named Chris Marsden. He lost his left thumb, but he was still alive. I found out later that the prize wheel for his next turn had landed on left leg. I had to wonder if he realized how lucky he was that we showed up when we did.

*****

The following day I spent at a cookout at my grandparents, who live in Pendleton, Indiana. They raised me after my parents died. Pops and grandma invited everybody. As the rest of the people enjoyed the swimming pool and a little basketball, Vernon and I sat bandaged and still sore from Spurling's takedown. That didn't stop us from enjoying the ribeye steaks that were pulled hot from the grill though. As I sat next to my best girl, Crystal, enjoying my steak, Zee sat down beside me.

"I'm kinda getting used to you saving my ass, Zee," I said shaking my head.

"Well, someone's gotta do it." Zee elbowed me in the side, and then kissed me on the forehead.

Zee had saved my life more than once, and she is one of my best friends. I couldn't do what I do, without Zee or Marty. All I can say is, I am one of the luckiest people in the world. I have a great family, I have great friends, and I have the most beautiful girl who is crazy enough to love me.

Learn more about the series:

Benjamin Kroh is the best the FBI's Behavioral Analysis Unit has to offer. Follow his exploits, along with his highly capable team, through the pages of his first novel, Die Laughing, and the sequel, Die by Proxy. Be on the lookout for more titles in the series coming soon!

About the Authors

Jason Cobalt was born in the Greater Detroit area and grew up in the coalfields of Appalachia. Cobalt is a former US Army officer, having served in two foreign wars. Jason's general interests include history, government and politics, business and finance, home brewing, shooting, working out, and rugby. He holds a Bachelor's in Business and a Masters in Government. Cobalt has also dabbled in yoga and hand-to-hand combat, but is not very good at them. He loves all dogs.

Contact Jason via email at authorjasoncobalt@gmail.com.

Charles Kelley grew up in the foothills of southern Indiana. He fled the farm lands upon graduation from high school to attend Ball State University. After receiving a B.S. in Criminal Justice/Criminology, he started his career working with various criminal justice agencies. His writing career started modestly with a personal blog, which developed his love of creative writing, leading to his web page of short stories. From there, he developed bigger ideas, starting with his Kings of Chaos Motorcycle Club Series. He currently resides in Indianapolis, Indiana and is trying his best to raise a family, further his career, and develop his writing skills.

You can find Charles online at the following links:
Website: www.ckfiction.com
Facebook: www.facebook.com/ckwriting
Instagram: www.instagram.com/ckfiction
Twitter: www.twitter.com/ckfiction
Email: authorcharleskelley@gmail.com

George Kramer started writing early in his life. In fifth grade, he started dabbling with his pen and paper. It was instrumental since his writing would serve as a crucial outlet later in life. The venting allowed him to get a handle on his trials and tribulations from growing up with eight other siblings.

George spread his wings and embraced writing in all genres. As it stands, he has over one hundred and fifty articles published online for various websites. He has written two books of unconventional poetry, countless short stories, and eight books of the popular Arcadis series. Additionally, he has written two medical horror books, Blind to Blood, and the sequel, Blind to Blood 2: The End Game, as well as a murder mystery called To Some It's Just a Rose. He has written screenplays for Blind to Blood, Arcadis: Prophecy, and To Some It's Just a Rose.

George was born in Brooklyn, NY, raised on Long Island, is one of nine children, and is a natural-born triplet. Currently, he resides in McCordsville, Indiana, with his wife and precocious daughter.

You can find George online at the following links:
Website: www.amazon.com/author/georgekramer
Facebook: https://www.facebook.com/george.kramer.50
Instagram: https://www.instagram.com/gkramer86/
Twitter: https://twitter.com/gkramer86
Email: georgekramerauthor@gmail.com

Cait Marie is the creator and manager of Functionally Fictional. Since 2017, she has held multiple positions within Coffee House Writers, including C.O.O., Advertising Supervisor, Editor, and Writer. In 2019, she joined the indie staff of YA Books Central as a reviewer and then Indie Assistant Blogger.

She graduated with honors in 2019 from Southern New Hampshire University with a Bachelor of Arts in psychology, and is currently considering pursuing a Master of Fine Arts degree in their Creative Writing program.

Cait lives in Indiana, where she freelance edits and provides a variety of other author services. When she's not writing or reading, she can usually be found watching Disney movies or *Brooklyn Nine-Nine*, painting, or singing along to showtunes.

Cait can be found online at the links below:
Website: https://caitmarieh.wordpress.com/
Functionally Fictional: https://functionallyfictional.com/
Facebook: https://www.facebook.com/cait.marie.h/
Facebook Group: https://www.facebook.com/groups/cait.maries.readers/
Instagram: https://www.instagram.com/c8_marie/
Twitter: https://twitter.com/c8_marie
Email: caitmarie.author@gmail.com

Adam K. Moore lives in Indianapolis, Indiana with his beautiful wife, his twin boys, and their dog, Stella. When he isn't writing stories, he's probably playing with his boys or engaged with one of his many hobbies. He grew up in a small town called Angola, Indiana, which he draws much of his inspiration from as settings for his stories. Adam and his friend, Charles Kelley, co-founded Circle City Publishing as a place for creative types to gather, create, and use the Oxford comma in their sentences like civilized humans.

Patrick J. O'Brian works as a full-time firefighter in Northeastern Indiana, writing and researching in his spare time. He writes primarily suspense thrillers and detective mysteries, though he has done a few arson mysteries.

He enjoys travel and visiting theme parks during the summer. He also does photography and dabbles in online auctions. At least once a year he travels to his home state of New York.

Find Patrick's website at www.pjobooks.com

Ben Oneal is an American fiction author, specifically crime thrillers. His works include "Die Laughing," and its sequel, "Die by Proxy."

He is the product of a barber and a telephone operator. Yes a man who could give a close shave as well as a haircut, and a woman on the other end of the phone, politely asking, "Number Please?"

He is a graduate of Purdue University with a degree in Industrial Illustration, and he found his career as a lamp designer for General Motors. It was there that he met a man who was as evil as any he creates in his stories. It was this experience that piqued his interest in criminal psychology, and in particular the broken mind of serial killers.

Ben is a lifelong seeker of knowledge and truth, and what he finds most abhorrent is a closed mind. He always enjoys the game, "What If".

Kathryn Schwarz is an aspiring author from Mississippi, USA. She enjoys writing short stories and working on the *Dragon's Ascent* series. She has a Tumblr page reserved solely for short stories that she's self-published (and where she likes to share writing memes), and she can be reached by curious askers there, or through her email.

Tumblr: http://zelsbels-writing.tumblr.com/
Email: d.a.blood.dragon@gmail.com

Christian Scully is the author of The Chronicles of Erika Lorenz series and related short stories. He started writing when he was fifteen and worked on several short films with friends. He attended Indiana State University and Indiana University of Kokomo for Communications with an emphasis on film studies. In 2010, he started writing novels and hasn't looked back.

When he's not writing, he's spending time with his wife, children, cat, and dog.

Christian can be found online at www.facebook.com/AuthorChristianScully/.

Make Your Mark.

Circle City Publishing

Our Story

Established in Indianapolis, Indiana in 2015 by writing partners Adam K. Moore and Charles Kelley to provide services to each other as well as other local, budding writers. Circle City Publishing aims to provide services such as full manuscript review (proofreading, editing, and critiquing), marketing and social media strategies, and assistance in finding the best printing options for every project.

Kelley and Moore are both self-published authors, who were unfamiliar with the writing and publishing processes when they sought out to begin their writing careers. Luckily, through each of their "on-the-job" trainings, they were able to piece things together step-by-step, and provide tips to each other along the way. Not wanting other first-time authors to feel lost or overwhelmed, Circle City Publishing was created to serve as a resource for other self-published writers. Their goal is to build a reliable writing community where knowledge can be pooled and used to benefit the collective.

The Logo

The city of Indianapolis was modeled after Washington D.C., with a circle in the heart of downtown, having roads split off in a spoke fashion; hence the nickname, the Circle City. It's only logical that our logo would be circular in nature then, right? In the middle of that circle in downtown Indianapolis is the Soldiers and Sailors Monument, and on top of that is the Lady Victory statue. It's a distinct feature of the city, so what better way to represent the Circle City than feature the iconic statue, front and center, in our logo? The fact that the design came directly from a collaboration with the founding members makes it that much better.

CPSIA information can be obtained
at www.ICGtesting.com
Printed in the USA
FSHW020454150320
68116FS